INSIGHT

A COLONY SIX NOVELLA

BOOKS BY TEYLA BRANTON

Colony Six
Insight
Sketches
Visions
Travels

Unbounded Series
The Change
The Cure
The Escape
The Reckoning
The Takeover

Unbounded Novellas
Ava's Revenge
Mortal Brother
Lethal Engagement
Set Ablaze

Imprints
First Touch
Touch of Rain
On the Hunt
Upstaged
Under Fire
Blinded

UNDER THE NAME RACHEL BRANTON

Lily's House
House Without Lies
Tell Me No Lies
Your Eyes Don't Lie
Hearts Never Lie
Broken Lies
No Secrets and Lies
Cowboys Can't Lie

Finding Home
All that I Love
Take Me Home

Other Books
How Far

INSIGHT

COLONY SIX BOOK 0

TEYLA BRANTON

WHITE
STAR
PRESS

This is a work of fiction, and the views expressed herein are the sole responsibility of the author. Likewise, certain characters, places, and incidents are the product of the author's imagination, and any resemblance to actual persons, living or dead, or actual events or locales, is entirely coincidental.

Insight (Colony Six, Book 0)

Published by White Star Press
P.O. Box 353
American Fork, Utah 84003

ISBN: 978-1-948982-08-5
Printed in the United States of America
Year of first printing: 2019

DEDICATION

For Sarah. Miss you, sis.

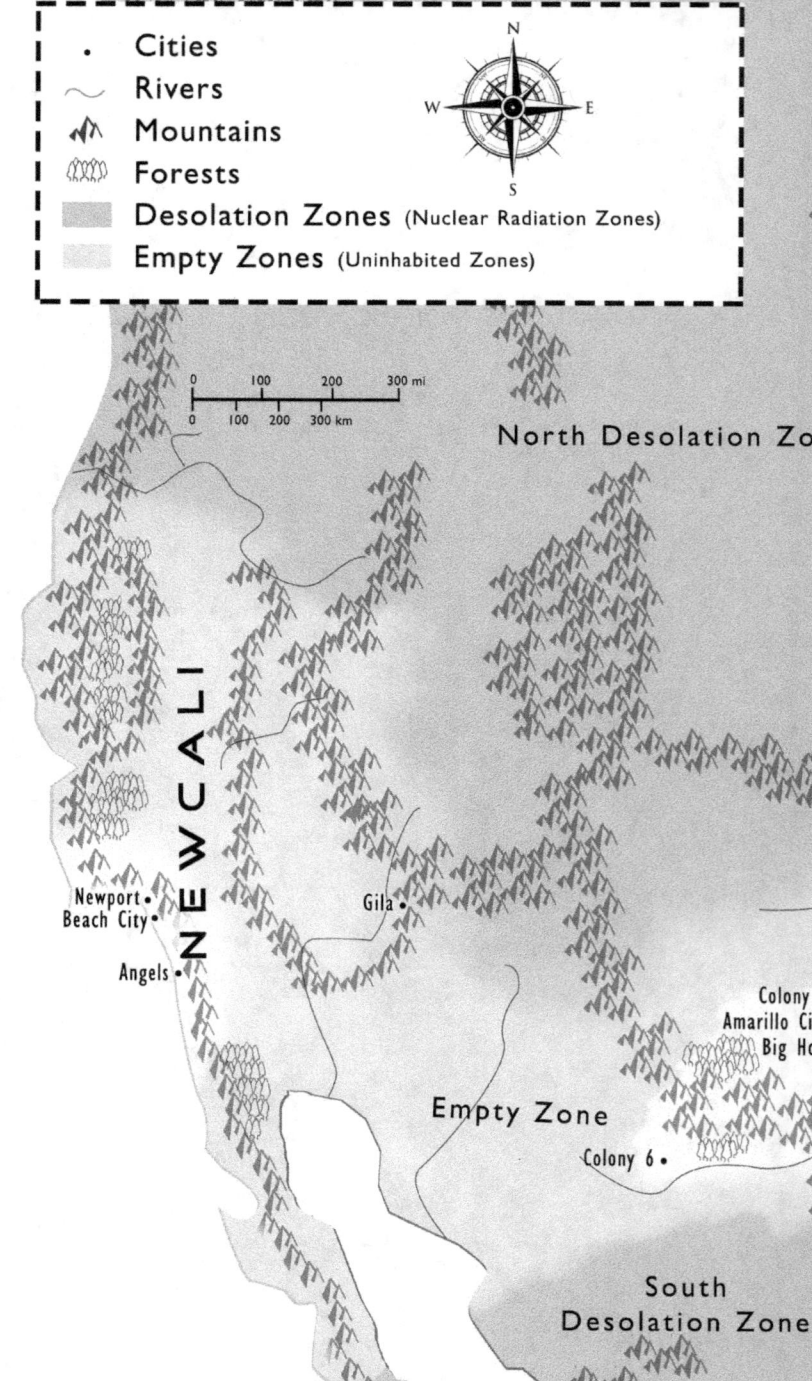

NOTE FROM THE AUTHOR

WELCOME TO THE CORE: COMMONWEALTH OBJECTIVE FOR REFORM AND EFFICIENCY

This novella is part of my *Colony Six* futuristic dystopian sci-fi series. After finishing the first two books, I decided I wanted to write about the catalyst that took Reese, one of my important characters, back to Dallastar near where she grew up and where the series really begins. This is the case that almost got her killed and eventually led to events that in subsequent books reunites her with her childhood crew from Welfare Colony 6, otherwise known as the Coop (after the cramped conditions and chickens they raised there for extra food).

You can read this story either before or after the other books in the series—it doesn't have spoilers. If you are new to my series, keep in mind that this short piece won't contain the intricacies of the much longer novels, but I hope it'll give you a taste of my post-apocalyptic world. I've included terms at the end of the novel to help catch you up, so maybe take a peek at those. Enjoy!

PROLOGUE

Location: Welfare Colony 6, Dallastar
Year: 2258, 60 years after Breakdown

The boys came running, laughing as they sped through the hallway on the way to lunch. Ten-year-old Reese Parker couldn't see them yet from her spot near the back door of their school wing, where she sat with her jean-covered legs stretched out in the sunlight that filtered through the glass, but she could hear their pounding footsteps as they came to meet her.

Here in this isolated place, they would never attract the attention of a more powerful crew, because doing so was only asking for trouble, even if most of the older kids were in a different wing and had other lunch periods. In a year or two, they might be strong enough to hold their own anywhere, especially with Dani around. For now, they were comparatively strong on their own in level ten.

Reese heard one of the boys trip—probably Jaxon, though it was Eagle who was practically blind. Eagle Eyes Jenson could remember each turn and navigated the hallways and classrooms at their school better than any of their crew. She set aside her precious sketchbook and looked up expectantly.

More laughter and an urgent shout. "Get up! Before he finds us!" Eagle's voice, not Jaxon's.

Sure enough, it was Eagle who turned the corner first and slid in beside her. His thin, freckled face held a wide smile, and his brown eyes under the heavy glasses were huge, magnified impossibly by the thick lenses. His brown hair was damp from exertion and hung limply in his eyes.

"What happened?" Reese asked, tossing him one of the readymeals she'd already snagged from the dispenser using his code. There were rumors about implanted codes that would force each child to collect their own meal, but adults talked about a lot of things that never happened. Reese figured by the time they got around to implanting IDs, she and her crew would be leveled out of school and away from the nightmare of living in the Coop.

Eagle caught the thin box with his scrawny arms and ripped off the plastic-coated carton top, grinning at the small bag of pretzels nestled in one of the small compartments. Reese was glad to see him so happy with his favorite snack. She had planned to give him hers if he didn't get any, because though the meals ran in cycles, you never really had a choice about what popped out.

He poked his finger in the thick sauce that covered chunks of what passed as meat but was really protein cubes of some sort. No one really knew. "Nice. Still hot."

Reese sighed impatiently. "You still haven't told me what happened. Why are you so late?" The boys always got out after she did when they had their physical education class, which was why she picked up their meals for them, but today they were even later than normal.

"Oh, you should have been there," Eagle said. "It was so fu—"

Whatever else Eagle tried to say was lost as Jaxon Crowley plowed around the corner and collapsed beside Reese. Part of his dark hair was wet with perspiration like Eagle's, and his blue eyes were dancing with the same amusement, but his face had an added gray tinge to it. A wide, red welt stood out on his neck.

"Did that pus licker zap you again?" Reese demanded, studying Jaxon's neck. He was her best friend, and she couldn't help the anger boiling up inside.

"Yeah." He swiped the back of his hand across his eyes, making his thick eyelashes stick together with moisture. "But this time we deserved it."

"Yep." Eagle nodded vigorously. "He caught us cutting out the soles of his shoes."

As Eagle spoke, a flash of an image came to Reese's mind. She saw the substitute teacher's florid face and shaved head, his heavy body rigid. Wrinkles gathered under his eyes, and an even deeper one ran down the bridge of his nose. A circle of dark, gray-flecked hair bordered his mouth, a mouth pursed as it screamed something that started with "You" as his finger jabbed out accusingly. His big ears were quickly turning red, along with his nose and the top of his head. That was a man ready to blow, and blow big.

Instinctively, Reese reached for her drawing pad, her fingers itching to get the image on paper. Instead, she brushed up against the two remaining readymeals. Taking a breath, she passed one to Jaxon, looking carefully to make sure he wasn't shaking. Stunners hurt bad, and though it was supposed to be illegal for anyone but enforcers to have them, there were more than a few at the school for secret use on recalcitrant students. But Jaxon's hand was steady, so whatever blast the teacher had managed to give him, it hadn't been all that powerful.

"He's going to kill you tomorrow." She hadn't seen the teacher except in her mind, but his angry face scared her. Maybe tomorrow the stunner wouldn't be on the lowest setting.

"Nope." Jaxon shook his head as he unhooked the plastic fork embedded in the side of the meal and dug in. "He was only here two days, and maybe wherever he goes next, he'll think twice about using a stunner to make boys run faster."

"Right!" Eagle licked off a bit of sauce that had fallen on his hand. "As if any of us are going to ever use what we learn in a physical education class."

"Running is important," Reese retorted.

Jaxon reached over to tug on one of her dark locks. "Yeah, but he can't teach us what we already know. We've been running from older crews since before we left nursery school."

"I guess." Reese scooped up her own readymeal. She wanted her drawing pad instead—her fingers tingled to draw the image in her mind. But she didn't like being compelled, as if something outside her had control, forcing her to record the images that had begun popping randomly into her mind. Images that were always one-hundred percent accurate. Jaxon knew about it, of course. She told him everything. He'd been born in the small house next to hers, six by seven meters like all the other houses in their district, and they'd been inseparable in nursery school, even before they'd formed a crew with Eagle and the others. A crew that kept them safe. But though he knew her secrets, she tried not to remind him of her weakness. Of the way she had to draw. Jaxon was the only halfway normal kid in their small crew of misfits, and he would be accepted into any other crew, but he'd chosen them. Because of her.

Pushing away the urge to draw, she leaned back against the metal door behind her that opened to stairs leading down into the bowels of the school. Eagle had once hacked into the hand-print lock, of course, and that was how they'd learned what the door hid—water pipes, electrical wiring, and furnaces. Furnaces that school officials rarely thought they needed in Welfare Colony 6, even though Reese remembered too many days when the inside of the school was colder than outside, and everyone wore extra sweaters and all the pants they owned and some of their parents' as well, if they were lucky enough to have them—both parents and pants, that is.

She moved her legs to catch more of the sunlight, refusing to think about that now. This was April and winter was too far away to worry about.

"So where are the girls?" Jaxon asked.

Reese shook her head. "Don't know." It worried her too that they were late, though it could have been the long lines at the readymeal dispensers. She hadn't seen them there as she normally did. She'd thought they'd already gone through, but they hadn't been waiting here for her.

"They'll be here soon," Eagle assured them.

Sure enough, they were still eating their meals when Dani Balak and the twins, Lyssa and Lyra Sloan, showed up. More freaks. The twins because they were twins and Dani because of her short spiky white hair and her very black skin. They carried readymeals but were running, Dani a good head taller than the petite twins.

"It's the Jammers!" Lyssa huffed.

Reese set aside her meal and jumped to her feet, her heart hammering inside her chest. The two Jammer brothers—Witt, an older boy, and Keag, who was their age—lived near them and were the meanest boys they knew. Their crew was mostly made up of the biggest kids in level twelve, some as big as Reese's father and as angry as him after he'd downed a skin of sauce. Witt was their leader, and the boys followed him around like dogs, swaggering and tormenting anyone who happened to be in their way.

"Saca!" Jaxon swore, fear making his voice tight. "What happened?"

"It's just Keag and some of their crew," Dani said, pushing her readymeal at Lyra and turning to face the bend where Reese could hear someone coming down the hallway. "Witt ain't with 'em. I can take care of it." She raised her fists into a ready position, an expression of gleeful anticipation on her square, rugged face. Her black skin glistened under the harsh hallway light. She looked fierce and more than a little unbalanced.

No doubt Dani could take Keag and a couple others at the same time, but Reese needed to be ready. She slipped her left hand into the pocket of her jeans and grasped the metal fork she'd stolen from the hospital last year after someone at the school had discovered her taking an important test with her non-dominant arm and realized her left was broken. Since the break thirteen months ago, she'd worked on using both hands, just in case. Both for school work and for fighting. Nothing was going to prevent her from leveling out of school and getting released from Colony 6. No way would she die working in the factories like her mother. She wanted to be out in the real world with the rest of the citizens in the CORE, instead of locked in with the poor trash that depended on charity to survive.

Next to Reese, Jaxon was also taking something from his pocket. She knew what it was without looking—a spoon he'd shaped to go over his knuckles. He hit almost as well as Dani. Even the twins and Eagle knew how to throw a punch. Well, with Eagle it was only if he managed to see where to land the punch, but he had a pretty good right hook, and his skinny arm was long and tough.

"If we fight, they'll know who we are!" Lyssa protested, her long ebony hair tied in braids on either side of her face. "If we hurt one of 'em, Witt will come after us."

"Then we fight!" Dani motioned for Lyssa to give her space.

"Why are they after you?" Reese switched her fork to her right hand, wiped her left on her pant leg and then switched the fork back to the left.

Lyra's slightly slanted dark eyes looked huge in her delicate face, a mirror image of her sister's. "They wanted my pretzels."

"You should have let them take the bag!" Lyssa growled at her. "It's not like they wanted your whole meal."

"But . . ." Lyra's eyes went to Eagle, who was standing behind Reese near the wooden door leading down into the basement. "I was saving them in case Eagle didn't get any."

Reese felt a little tug in her chest, but it didn't surprise her that Lyra would refuse a dominant crew something meant for Eagle. Their crew was as close as family. Or closer in her case.

"I just started running," Lyra continued. "I thought I'd lost them for a while, but they followed me here. They aren't very fast, so I caught up with Dani and Lyssa and told them to run."

"You did right to refuse them," Dani said through gritted teeth. "We can't let them take anything that's ours. That will make them target us more. We can fight them."

"Or we could disappear," Eagle said.

Glancing over her shoulder, Reese saw that Eagle had the combination pad to the door dismantled and the door to the basement was open. Eagle shrugged as he clicked the panel over the wires. "It's easy after you do it the first time. I remembered how."

Of course he did. Just as he knew how many steps were in each hallway and classroom. It was his version of using both hands. His mind, or maybe his memory, was his ticket to leveling out of school, despite the poor vision that might ordinarily cause him to fail.

"Yes, let's go!" Lyssa urged, focusing her attention primarily on Dani. "If we fight, they'll remember us. But if we hide, maybe they won't. We weren't with Lyra when it happened. They might not know she's a twin. And if they see you now, they'll never forget you. You're the only one with that skin color and hair. They won't rest until they kill us all."

"We can take them," Dani insisted.

"Yeah, but Witt and the others too?" Eagle asked. "And for how long? What if they catch some of us alone?"

The six kids stared at each other for a moment, all the while listening to the approaching footsteps that had slowed as the opposing crew obviously checked classrooms and other hall-ways. Not for the first time, Reese wondered if their choices would be different if they weren't all freaks.

"Eagle and Lyssa are right," Reese said, so everyone knew where she stood. She wasn't afraid to fight when she had to, but fighting when there was a safer option, especially for the twins and Eagle, was pure stupidity.

Jaxon met Dani's eyes. He was officially their leader and normally influenced their final decisions, but Dani was a wild card. If she wanted to fight, they'd fight. Not one of them would leave her.

Dani heaved a sigh. "Fine. But only because the twins have too many classes without me. I swear on the head of my grand-mother, one of these days, I'm going to teach those pus-licking, warthog-faced, punk buckets all a lesson."

Reese shuddered at the threat. She didn't envy the Jammers. In the past two years, Dani had gone from a regular girl to a fighting machine. She moved faster than seemed possible, and her punches had already laid out more than a few older kids. In a year or two, no other crew would be able to mess with them, not even those in the eighteenth level.

Dani stood guard while they gathered up their readymeals and darted inside. A dim glow shone in the stairwell far below, and Reese was glad for the light. The door locked behind them with an automated click. Eagle sat on the first stair and the others followed. Only Dani remained standing by the closed door, ready for anything.

Almost immediately, taunting voices filled the hallway, and someone banged on the door to the basement when they realized it was locked.

"That just goes to the basement," came a voice. "No one can get down there but the janitor."

"They must have gone outside," said someone else. "Come on. We'll get them out there." Shuffled steps moved away.

"They'll be opening the door right . . . about . . . now," Eagle whispered. Sure enough, they heard a loud *thwack!* as someone roughly pushed on the outside door.

"They'll have to be in class soon," Lyssa said. "They can't lurk around our hallways much longer." Lyra nodded in agreement.

"We've got time to finish eating," Jaxon lifted the carton top covering his meal.

Now that they were no longer in immediate danger, Reese's hands itched to draw again. She had to draw the face of the substitute teacher. Her stomach ached with the need.

"You going to eat those?" Eagle pointed at her pretzels.

"No. Go ahead." She tossed them at him. Lyra tossed hers at him too, followed by Lyssa and Jaxon.

Dani aimed her bag at Eagle's head, laughing and shaking her head, the white strands of her hair poking out crazily. "You deserve them," she said, hitting him on the forehead.

Ten minutes later they were heading to math class, the one class they all had together. By then Reese was sweating and shaking.

She had to draw the image of the teacher she'd seen from Eagle's mind, but it wasn't as though she could mask what she was doing. They used Teevs embedded in their desks, and all schoolwork was submitted electronically. The only exception was art class. In math class, the teacher would notice her scribbling, maybe even take away her precious pad and drawing pencils, the only things of value she owned, a gift from her father's aunt on the outside. She'd filled the other pads already, and this one still had so many fresh white pages.

Jaxon nudged up against her as they entered the room. "Whatever you need to draw, do it," he whispered. "Sit behind me. I'll get Old Geyser talking. He won't even notice you sketching."

Reese nodded, unable to speak. If she didn't get it out, she'd be shaking the rest of the day, and that wasn't good. She couldn't afford to fail.

She slid into a seat behind Jaxon and pulled her drawing pad out of her ragged sack. In minutes, the sketch of the substitute teacher appeared under her hand, as if of its own volition. She was aware of each line, each curve, each bit of shading, as if it were a part of her—and yet somehow coming from outside. She didn't need her eraser once. She wished she could use some of the colored pencils she'd permanently "borrowed" from her art class, but those were at home, tucked under her CORE-issued mattress. She shaded the redness of the man's face with her pencil instead.

Relief filled her as the urge to sketch drained away. The result wasn't her best drawing ever, but close. Someone tapped her on the shoulder, and she turned to see a scrawny boy she didn't know well sitting next to her, his head craned to see her drawing. "You got his face exactly right," he whispered. "So glad that pus bag was only here for two days."

Nodding in agreement, she gave the boy a smile and shut her drawing pad, tucking it under her. At the front of the classroom, the math teacher paced back and forth, waving his hands animatedly in the air to emphasize his story about the usefulness of math in every profession. Jaxon glanced back at her and winked. He wouldn't ask about the picture later, and she wouldn't remind him. This was why he was her best friend.

He would always be. Nothing could separate them. Not even leaving the Coop.

Except in the end, it didn't work out that way. Not even a little.

CHAPTER 1

Location: Amarillo City, Estlantic
Year: 2278, 80 years after Breakdown

Detective Reese Parker began recording the sketch, her hand moving quickly over her drawing pad. She ignored the prisoner, Arlie Cruz, seated across the table with his cuffed arms folded up to his bony chest in a way that clearly said he wasn't going to tell her anything.

But he already had. More than he could ever guess.

A man's image formed under her fingers. The blunt curve of his jowly face, the lumpy nose, the swollen, pouty lips. The hair that was short in front and touched the material of his collarless suit in the back. His ears were large for even his decidedly hefty proportions. He wasn't a handsome man by any stretch of the imagination, though he might have been in his younger years, but he exuded power and confidence. The smoothness around his brown eyes testified of Nuface therapy, and he'd probably had it more than once. Yet weight and age had caught up to him in the end, showing in the puffy, saggy cheeks and the uneven nose. His chest was also heavy above his comparatively slender legs, in that way men sometimes got as they aged and ate in too many restaurants instead of sticking to the filling and nutritionally balanced readymeals.

What she didn't know yet was how the man in her drawing related to the man seated in front of her and the juke they'd found in the destroyed building.

"What are you doing?" demanded the prisoner, craning his thin neck to see her drawing, but Reese kept the pad angled so he couldn't see it.

She was also careful to keep it out of direct line of the room's camera. Anyone watching her interrogation would assume she was simply preparing her canvas with a blank character, similar to those in Teev-generated identification programs. Because that was what she'd told them in the past. After all, she couldn't possibly sketch a suspect that hadn't yet been verbally described. Her coworkers already thought she was strange to work with paper and pencil, which was far more costly than using a Teev and its elaborate software, but the ninety-nine percent identification rate from her drawings had given her leeway with Captain Homer. He complained about the cost of paper, though, and these days she bought as much on her own as she ordered from division. Too many of the sketches she received from those around her had nothing to do with enforcer business. She'd grown accustomed to carrying a personal notepad along with her official one.

She let her prisoner stew for a moment, her pencil shading in the man's suit. It was black with silver threads woven throughout, but she couldn't tell from the drawing if it was a name brand outfit or one of the cheap knockoffs. Probably it was real. He also had a thick gold chain around his wrist and a heavy gold ring.

"I'm waiting for you to tell me what you were doing in that

building, Mr. Cruz," she said finally. "I know you're selling juke."

"I have no idea what you're talking about," Cruz retorted, one corner of his narrow lips lifting in a mocking sneer. With his small eyes, pinched mouth, and pointed nose, he was completely unlike the man in her drawing. More like a ferret she'd seen on a pre-Breakdown animal show.

"Why don't I believe that?" Reese said mildly.

"Look, I was just poking around and that building seemed interesting," he continued. "That's all. It ain't a crime to investigate an empty zone, is it? Not yet anyway. Does that kid even claim to know me? If he does, where's his proof?"

"We found the juke," Reese reminded him, looking up at Cruz but not stopping her sketch.

"Are my prints on it? My DNA?" Cruz snorted, his mean little eyes triumphant. "You don't have anything on me. I'm an honest, hard-working man with a wife and kid."

He was right. Not about the honest part, but she didn't have anything solid on him. For weeks, she and her partner had been following a student from a Teev certificate institute, a twenty-year-old kid known for selling smeg laced with juke. On its own the mildly addictive smeg, a drug that simulated a sexual rush, wasn't illegal, but mixed with the harder juke, it had a devastating effect on CORE youth. Today the student had led them to a dilapidated building in an empty zone, and Reese had been sure they'd finally followed the tiny fish to a medium-sized fish, and somehow, by CORE, she was going to find the daddy fish.

The problem was, there was no direct Teev feed in most of the empty zones, and Reese and her partner had to go in blind. The result was that while juke was present at the house, they had nothing substantial to connect it to Cruz. Even the student denied knowing him, saying Cruz wasn't his usual contact, and nothing on the drugs themselves showed any link to Cruz. Captain Homer had already sent the boy to reconditioning. It was his first offense, so a little education might turn him around. If not, his next stop would be banishment to a colony or permanent medical enhancement. Usually the colony threat was enough to turn around anyone who wasn't addicted to juke.

"So when are you going to let me go?" Cruz demanded. "You can't hold me."

He was right about that too, but Reese wasn't willing to admit defeat. At least not yet. When she'd asked Cruz where he'd gotten the drugs, his mind had clearly sent her the flash of the man in her drawing. A flash she called a sketch. Without realizing it, Cruz had identified whoever was over him, but since their conversation was being recorded by the cameras in the room, she had to get him to verbalize a description before she could act on the drawing.

"Okay," she said. "Let's go through it again. What were you doing there?" It wasn't the first time for the question, but she wanted to see if he gave the same answer. "It's the middle of the day. On a Tuesday. Shouldn't you be at work?"

Cruz worked for Kordell Corp, or the KC as it was often referred to. The company was the largest non-CORE-owned business in Estlantic, and they created and packaged ready-meals. Their largest single client was the CORE itself, and the company supplied most of the charity units donated to the six welfare colonies. With three hundred thousand of the CORE's two million citizens confined to the colonies because of their inability to support themselves, that was significant. The colony contract alone meant Kordell Corp received a lion's share of the fifty percent taxes levied on both the CORE population and businesses alike. But while the KC was impressive, Cruz was just a low-level manager, and Reese was nowhere close to determining if he was acting on his own or if the company was also involved. The more she thought about it, the more ready-meal packaging seemed a perfect front for a drug operation.

"I told you." Cruz's tone was aggrieved. "My girl, she's into pre-Breakdown history, and her birthday's next week. I went to the empty zone to see if I could find something. I thought I'd better do it before they make them off limits altogether. Rumors say that's next."

The way he said it was angry and indignant, and Reese recognized the not-so-subtle hint that his loyalty to the CORE might not be complete. If the Elite made the empty zones off limits, it might reduce the amount of pre-Breakdown tech turned in, but it would make her job easier, not to mention protect people from any of the radiation-crazed monsters from the desolation zones.

"Why go so far northwest?" she asked. "That's getting close to the North Desolation Zone. You know the radiation there is dangerous."

"Right, but everything closer's been picked clean," he growled. "Everyone knows if you want to discover something valuable, you have to do a little footwork."

"Why that particular building?"

He shrugged. "It looked more intact than the others. And big. I thought it might have a basement. Office buildings sometimes have interesting equipment."

"You know all technology must be turned into our office."

"Yeah, yeah. I didn't mean that. I meant furniture or a picture." He leaned forward suddenly. "Or maybe some of those pencils and notebooks like you got there."

It was much the same story he'd given her before, with only nonconsequential variations. Nothing she could lever to make him rat on whoever pulled his chain. She knew he was guilty, and that he knew far more than he was saying, but unless she requested truth drugs, he might not tell her anything. And those cases were always transferred to the Headquarters Enforcer Division, or HED, to be overseen by the Controller himself.

"Okay," she said, leaning back and taking the drawing pad with her, still careful to protect it until Cruz gave her the pertinent information. "Maybe you aren't involved, but you've got eyes. If you're not responsible for the drugs, someone else was in that building. Did you see anyone?"

"Just that kid."

"Right. But what about before you reached the building? Surveillance at the edge of that particular empty zone didn't show anyone else entering where you did." This was a lie, but Cruz had no way of knowing that. There had been exactly six other people entering, and her partner was currently tracking them all, but at first glance none of them seemed likely. "You were there searching, obviously, for your daughter's birthday gift. You might have seen someone else. The drugs had to get there somehow, so if you saw even a glimpse of someone else, that might go a long way to corroborating your story. And helping me identify him would protect children like your daughter."

Would he jump at the bait?

"Now that you mention it, there was someone," he said hesitantly. "But I only saw him once a few minutes away from the building."

She nodded. "Good. Okay, that's a start." Now she had to make him describe the person in her sketch. And that meant leading questions, not waiting for him to come up with his own lie.

"So, did he have long hair or short in the front? I hope short, so you can tell me the color of his eyes."

"Yeah, short. Above the eyes." Cruz relaxed in his chair, letting his hands drop to his lap.

"So longer in the back, if the front was short? Brown hair and eyes, like ninety percent of the population?"

"Right," he said. A slight smirk hovered around his mouth for a second. He thought he was being smart, and Reese didn't mind letting him believe he was playing her. She was more convinced than ever that he hadn't seen anyone besides the student in the empty zone, not even the man in her drawing. But the man in the drawing was somehow connected to Cruz and the drugs.

She shaded a little more on the image, as if concentrating. In reality, she was filling in the background, a darkened room with only hazy features. Nothing really identifiable. "Was his nose smooth, or was it the kind that might be more lumpy from being broken? A guy like that has probably been in a lot of fights."

"Oh, lumpy," he said quickly. "I'll bet he's even been detained by enforcers before. He's probably in the database."

Everyone's in the database, Reese wanted to sneer at him but somehow manage to refrain. "Older man then, with some experience under his belt?"

"Yeah, yeah. Real strong."

And so she led him along the trail she needed him to go. Each feature he identified could have been the base for tens of thousands of other people in the CORE, but they also fit the man in her drawing. Only another sketch artist would catch what she was doing or wonder how she came up with details in her final sketch, but she was the only artist in this division. Most enforcer artists worked for the Central Identification Unit and were called temporarily to different divisions as needed. The CIU was always trying to recruit her, but she'd wanted to do more than just draw. So for the past ten years she'd clawed her way up the enforcer ladder to detective status, and she wasn't about to give that up. Maybe someday the skills she was learning would help her solve the murders from her past.

Cruz was talking again, asking when he could be released, but she held up a finger. "Just a minute. I'm almost finished. And I'll need to show you the sketch before you leave." But she needed one more thing first—a background of sorts that might lead to an identifiable location. She carefully phrased her next question, hoping his mind would automatically focus on the real man behind the drugs. "Where exactly did you see him? This man responsible for the drugs. What did the building he was near or in look like?"

Cruz cleared his throat, as if stalling for time. Too late for him. A sketch of the same man as before flashed to Reese's mind. This time he was inside a large factory of some kind. Behind him to each side, two lines of workers, dressed in white from head-to-toe, stood at tables scattered with juke hypos.

"Uh, just out in the rubble," Cruz said, coming to life as if aware that his reaction was too telling. "You know, tangled metal, chunks of concrete. I didn't really see him for long." He shook his head. "I'm sure whatever I've told you won't solve anything. I'm really sorry."

Reese didn't have time then to put the second sketch into her book, but it would remain crystal clear in her mind until she did. In fact, it would gnaw away at her until she recorded it, but she could wait without shaking, as long as there weren't too many images piled up in her brain.

"Thanks," she told Cruz. "You've been a big help. Let's get this into the Teev and run a search."

"Don't I get to see it?"

"Of course." She smiled and extended her pad.

Cruz leaned forward and gave an audible gasp. Color leaked from his face, leaving him pasty. "No!" he grated. "That's not him. I don't know that man! I didn't see *him*!" The words came with a strange panting breath.

"But you said you did."

"No!" His reply was strangled, and with it came another sketch to Reese's mind. A flash of a dead man lying on a floor, a bullet hole through his temple. The image sent a shudder through her body.

One thing was clear: whoever the man in the sketch was, selling juke was the least of his crimes.

CHAPTER 2

Cruz lurched to his feet and brought up his cuffed hands, jabbing one finger down on the man's face. "He. Was. Not. There. That man is nothing like the one I described."

The door slammed open and two enforcers entered the interrogation room, weapons drawn. "Sit down," one of them barked. "No sudden moves, or we'll shoot."

"But it's not him. It's not!"

Reese grabbed the cuffs holding Cruz's hands and lifted them enough to pull her drawing pad away. She still had to scan this in properly, though the cameras in the room would have already recorded it by now.

"On the contrary," she said. "You described him perfectly. And I'm sure our database will be able to find him."

"But—"

"I said sit down!" One of the enforcers yanked Cruz back into his seat.

Cruz stayed in place with his mouth shut and his eyes wide, as if stunned into silence.

Reese studied him. He was not only afraid, but mortally afraid. That meant her drawing was important. "If it's not correct," she consoled him, "I'm sure the database won't find anything."

A suppressed sob burst from his throat. Gone was his mocking confidence. His impatience. He looked beaten and terrified. Reese exchanged a glance with her fellow enforcers near the door. The men were younger than she was, standard beat enforcers, Neil Sumas and Mack Riding. They both had brown hair and eyes, but Neil's pug nose was dusted with freckles and Mack, the taller of the two, had a long face that made him look too thin. Underneath their surprise was a hint of amusement.

Reese wasn't amused. Instead, she felt a sliver of sorrow for the man. But whatever he was hiding was big, and she couldn't let it go. She was debating the likelihood of getting anything more from him when he gulped and stood up, nearly knocking his chair over. Neil and Mack took a step forward, weapons aimed purposefully at his heart.

"Sit down," Reese growled at Cruz, hoping he wasn't planning on getting himself killed. Because the wild glint in his eyes told her he was beyond caution. He probably didn't even hear her order.

"Stunners only," she barked at the enforcers. Cuffed as Cruz was, he wasn't much of a challenge for any of them, and she didn't want him killed accidentally. Sheepishly, the enforcers drew their stunners instead. At least now they wouldn't shoot him before she figured out his secret.

"I did it," Cruz said into the abrupt silence. "I brought the juke there and met the boy instead of the usual courier. I was going to make him an offer of a promotion. He's been a good dealer. I'm guilty." He stared into Reese's eyes, pleading. "And I want to make amends. Please, I'll go through reconditioning. I know I was wrong."

"Sit down," Reese repeated. For a moment, Cruz didn't obey, though it wasn't from belligerence. It was as if he needed those seconds to process her command, as if the shock to his system had changed him somehow.

"You know that psychological reconditioning isn't likely on the table," she said when he was seated, "not with the charges against you. You're looking more at medical enhancement or internment at a colony."

He grabbed on that. "Yes. I'll go to a colony and work there. I want to pay for what I've done."

"For an honest, hard-working husband and father, you certainly seem willing to abandon your wife and child."

"Of course I don't want to leave them!" His features twisted in anguish.

"Then maybe if you give us this man . . ." She tapped the drawing.

Cruz shook his head wildly. "I don't know him! Look, I did it. I'll tell you everything you want to know. Everything. I'll give you my distributors. My warehouse. Everything. Send me to a colony if you have to. But I don't know that man!"

Cruz was obviously more afraid of the man in the drawing than he was of her or any punishment the CORE could dish out. Instead of arguing, Reese nodded slowly. "I need more details to be sure you're telling the truth."

"It's juke," Cruz panted, "but I manufacture it with smeg. It gets people addicted faster."

All doubt that he was involved vanished with those details. "All right. I'll need the names of your dealers and the location of your factory." She unclipped her iTeev from her uniform sleeve and brought up her notepad, even though the camera would record everything.

Cruz looked at her blankly, then regained some of his former confidence. "I want an advocate first," he said.

The request wasn't customary, but given that his life was at stake, she supposed she would have to appoint him an advocate to argue in his behalf. He'd already admitted guilt, but he might still wrangle his way out of enhancement or being sent to a colony, though she doubted it. Most advocates were, after all, employed by the CORE, and the Director's office was never lenient on juke runners. But it meant her job was done, and she was fine handing him over to one of her colleagues. At the moment, she was far more interested in the man from the sketch.

"Okay." She motioned to the other enforcers. "Take him back to his cell and notify an advocate."

"Wait, can I call my work?" Cruz asked.

She blinked at him. "Your work, not your wife?"

He shrugged. "I got people who work under me. They'll contact her."

Reese supposed even a low-level manager at Kordell Corp had a secretary. Something nagged at her mind, and she paused to think about it. The second sketch she'd received from Cruz put the man in her first drawing in a factory surrounded by white-clad people. They could be readymeal packers. Could it have been food-packing paraphernalia and not drug hypos on the tables? She didn't think so, but she wouldn't know until she sketched it out and ran it through the Teev database.

"Notify his office," she said to the enforcers. "But no details, please. His factory might be on their property."

"They're not involved!" Cruz blurted. "I swear."

"Get him out of here."

The enforcers grabbed his arms and pushed him from the room. Sweeping up her pad from the table, Reese put it in her bag and hurried after them, keeping a few meters away. She'd learned a lot about control over the past year, and most of the time when she didn't have a sketchbook in hand, she no longer glimpsed her colleagues' secrets. But today she was already feeling exhausted and that meant her resistance was low, and she'd rather not catch a glimpse into their personal lives.

As she entered her office, a tiny room with barely enough space for her desk, the screens on the wall came alive with images—three depicting her upscale apartment and one of the beach. It was so real, sometimes she forgot and tried to walk into her kitchen.

With an upward motion of her hands, she brought her Teev display to life, hovering over her desk. "Bring up the identification program," she said.

The program immediately appeared on the holoscreen. Placing her drawing of the mystery man under it, she directed the Teev to scan. Once it was uploaded to her program, she went to work, using a narrow brush to give the man added dimension and color. When that was complete, she started a search for a human match in the enforcer database.

While the Teev worked, Reese brought out her personal drawing pad and sketched the other images she'd received from Cruz's brain. But aside from the apparent factory background and people dressed in white working hard at their stations in the second sketch, there wasn't anything to identify the place. Even the building that could be seen through the window wasn't unique. It could have been any of the post-Breakdown buildings in New York. The only suspicious part of the sketch were the very obvious hypos on the workers' tables.

The third image, the one of the dead man, was more promising only because the face was clear, even under the blood, which she could easily omit. She should be able to get an ID, though she wouldn't be able to officially connect it with her case, not unless she interviewed Cruz again and got him to admit he'd seen a dead man. She wasn't going to hold her breath on that happening.

She'd uploaded the new drawings to her private database, removed the blood, enhanced the color, and started a search to identify the dead man when the Teev beeped a signal that told her someone was outside her door.

"Come in," she said, shutting her sketchpad and giving the Teev a signal to end the holo display over her desk.

Her partner, Bay Danvers, strode into the room, his bulk making the doorway look small. His wide face was typically flushed with effort, and today was no exception. Despite his sagging paunch, he had strong arms and massive hands that packed a hard punch. He couldn't run nearly as fast as she could, but what he lacked in that area, he more than made up for in experience. His black uniform fit too tightly, and she wished, not for the first time, that he'd go up a size. It was a pride issue, she guessed. Bay had hit forty recently, which made him ten years older than Reese. As far as partners went, he was the best she'd had.

"We were right," he said without preamble. "The others we traced going to that area of the empty zone were all back before Cruz."

"I've no doubt he's our man," Reese said. "He knew the juke was mixed with smeg. Did you hear he asked for an advocate?"

Bay snorted as he leaned against the wall with her beach scene. It was strange seeing the apparent air hold his weight. "I heard, and he's already shown up."

Reese blinked. "That was fast."

"He says he's been engaged by Kordell Corp. He was apparently on his way before we called."

"No way," Reese muttered. Private advocates were customarily used only by Elites or their relatives. "Why would Kordell Corp care that much about him?"

Bay's big shoulders lifted in a shrug. "Maybe they're worried he's using company property."

"Right. They'll be protecting themselves. It certainly won't do him any good. He confessed."

"I also heard he went back on his identification."

"Too late. I'm searching the database." She grinned at him. "We're going fishing."

He gave a hearty chuckle, and a flash came to her—of Bay on a dock with a fishing pole. There was only one section of ocean that was safe for fishing, and each fish had to be tested for radiation even then, so Reese recognized the dock. She gave an internal sigh. One more sketch she'd have to get out on paper before she'd be able to sleep tonight.

Bay was about to speak when her Teev beat him to it. "Identification successful," it chimed.

Reese lifted her hands to restart the display. There poised above her desk was the man in her first sketch from Cruz. He was Tadum Grogovit, an executive officer and part owner of Kordell Corp.

She must have gasped because Bay, at an angle to the image, lumbered around the desk to stare at the man. He whistled, his color deepening with excitement. "This is big. I've heard they're connected to the underground."

Reese had heard the same thing but had put it down to envy. Now she wasn't so sure. This man had come to Cruz's mind when she'd asked about his supplier, and if the KC was involved in drugs, they might be connected to the underground as well.

"No wonder Cruz reneged on his identification," Bay said. "This guy has power. He's one of the few non-Elite who does."

"Let's see where Mr. Grogovit is right now." Reese brought up her holo keyboard and typed in the request. Implanted CivIDs had been mandatory in Estlantic for five years now, so if Grogovit was close to any camera that connected to the Teev feed, she'd be able to track him.

The words *Current Location Unknown* flashed on the screen.

"Let's review recordings from earlier." Bay hunched closer to the holoscreen, as anxious as she was to see the information. "Narrow it around the Kordell corporate office. He's got to be there."

Reese put in the commands. "Looks like he arrived at ten. There's a record of him entering the parking garage next to the building. He has a personal car that he parks in the section rented out to private citizens. No sign of him leaving, though. The last time he connected to the feed on his iTeev or any other personal device was at four. It's only five. Most people here might work only six hours a day, but he's an executive. He's probably still there."

Bay grinned at her. "Let's go pick him up."

"Wait." Reese pushed the option to send the information to her portable iTeev before sitting back and staring up at her partner. "Let's think a minute."

"Your drawing is enough to bring him in," Bay said. "Even him. At least for questioning."

"I know, but if we don't find evidence, and Cruz continues to deny the identification, nothing will stick. I want more."

Bay laughed. "That's what my wife always says every time we go see another apartment."

After ten years of applications, Bay and his wife had been awarded a birth order last month, and his newly pregnant wife wanted a bigger place for when their baby was born. On another day, Reese would have laughed and teased him about his pending fatherhood, but she was too intent on the juke factory and the dead man in her other sketch. She believed that Grogovit was involved in both, but if they picked him up without more proof, they might never find the factory or proof that he'd killed someone.

"He's got a lot of money," she said. "And knowing he's the

man in the sketch answers why Cruz already has a private advocate here. We need more on this guy." Reese hated to admit it, but she suspected money and power might elude justice, even in the CORE.

Bay nodded. "I see what you mean."

"If the company is involved, they won't simply give us what we want. More likely, they'll give us a fake location or one of their smaller factories to connect with Cruz. I'm thinking maybe Grogovit will get anxious when he hears that Cruz has confessed, and Grogovit will lead us somewhere better."

"Sounds like stakeout time to me," Bay said. "Thank the CORE I don't have to go see another apartment tonight. I'll grab some snacks and let my wife know we're working late. You order the shuttle. Oh, and make sure the Teev notifies us if he leaves his building."

Reese motioned the holo keyboard closer to her and began tapping. "Got it. I'll meet you in the shuttle bay in ten."

CHAPTER 3

B ay had no sooner left when the Teev finished the second
identification. The dead man had been found naked in the
river near her division. There had been no arrest and no clues
about who had put him there. His name was Dane Crowley.

Reese felt a catch in her chest at the name. Crowley had
been Jaxon's last name, her best friend from Colony 6. After
his mother had died, Jaxon disappeared from the colony, as all
orphaned children did. Abandoned by her father, Reese herself
ended up on the outside in her great-aunt's care a short time
later. She'd never seen Jaxon or any of the others again.

After becoming an enforcer, she'd used their database to
search his name. Nothing. She'd looked the others up too, but
Eagle had gone by a nickname, and she couldn't remember
Dani or the twins' full names. When she attempted to search
Colony 6 school records, her access was denied, and her quest
had ended there.

Or almost. Two years out of the enforcer academy, she'd
begun dating a guy in personnel in the hopes of discovering

more information. That attempt ended in a nasty breakup when he'd caught her drawing a sketch from his mind. Two days later, she'd been forced into psychiatric care with a doctor that had resulted in months under a microscope.

If a decade in Colony 6 had taught her anything, it was that you don't stand out, and you never admit to anything. After three months of regular appointments, the doctor gave her a release. Needless to say, her relationship with the personnel officer didn't work out, and she'd hidden her ability ever since. She believed in the CORE and its goal, but she'd seen a few innocents suffer over the course of her career, and she wasn't going to be one of them.

She hoped her friends had been able to get out of the colony like she had, but she'd come to terms with the fact that maybe she'd never know. This didn't mean she didn't have regrets, because she did. Huge ones. A part of the girl she'd been had died with the loss of her crew, and she'd never been able to replace any of them. Bay was the best partner she'd ever had, but he had no clue about growing up in the Coop, and she couldn't tell him, not in any way that did the experience justice.

After alerting the shuttle bay that she needed a shuttle instead of her usual scrambler, she sketched the image she'd glimpsed of Bay on the dock in her personal notebook, and then packed both her notebooks into her special bag. Next, she went to her private dressing cubicle in outfitting, where she made sure she had her Enforce nine mil, a backup Enforce .380, a temper laser, a stunner, and extra cartridges. All the weapons were programmed to her fingerprints. She also carried a knife that wasn't approved by division. Maybe it was her time in the colony, but she was never without it. After tucking all her weapons into the pockets and built-in holsters in her black uniform—or her blues as they were called—she was ready to take on anything.

Even Kordell Corp? A shiver of unease crawled over her shoulders.

Yes, even them, she decided. The KC was powerful, but she was an enforcer doing her job, and she had the CORE backing her.

Pushing aside her misgivings, Reese gave her assault rifle a longing glance before leaving her dressing cubicle. She'd be better off calling for backup, if something like that came into play. Grogovit might have set up a drug-running operation, but guns were harder to get in the underground, and if there was a confrontation, what she carried should be enough.

Maybe.

Tossing her thoughts aside, she hurried to the shuttle bay where a silver, tetrahedron-shaped shuttle with red and black enforcer stripes already awaited. Unlike the public shuttles that were normally a calming blue and always driven by Teev, the enforcer shuttles were faster, the metal tops could fold back inside the rear compartment, and they had optional manual controls.

Reese kicked at the wheel and shook her head at the attendant. "No, Warren, I said it was for surveillance. We'd be identified in an instant if we showed up in this."

Warren ran a hand through his long black hair. "Oh, right. Sorry. I'll just be a minute."

As he lumbered off, Reese gave a longing look at the rows of two-wheeled aerodynamic scramblers which were her normal transportation. Most citizens used the solar sky trains, which was pre-Breakdown tech, but everyone had an allotment of public shuttle rides each month, and enough of the wealthy owned cars as well, so that meant some days there was a lot of traffic in the city. A scrambler could bypass much of that while on patrol. Best of all, the pre-Breakdown tech ran on fuel cells that could be used for a month without refueling. Reese might have grown bored with her job, but she'd never grow bored of riding a scrambler.

Except today for once she wasn't bored with her job. This was big. Life-changing maybe. She personally didn't care about climbing any corporate ladder, and she had no interest in joining the Controller's Special Forces, but this could be good for Bay and his family.

Warren returned with a small blue shuttle at the same time Bay appeared, loaded with a huge black duffel, most of which she guessed was stuffed with food. Fifteen minutes later, she and Bay were parked outside the main offices of Kordell Corp.

They waited. Or rather, Reese did while Bay ate dinner and dessert and a few snacks. Leaving her readymeal untouched on her lap, she removed her iTeev from her sleeve, unfolding the square and extricating the ear supports to put it over her face like glasses, feeling it settle and mold to the curves of her face. She brought up her own holoscreen, one that only she could see unless Bay was wearing his own iTeev and she broadcast what she was doing to him. Which she wouldn't do. He didn't know about the second image of Grogovit, and she couldn't exactly tell him without coming up with a plausible story first. Not for the first time, she wished she'd mastered the iTeev's more private eye movement navigation, but like most of the CORE residents, she preferred using hand motions or voice commands to interact with the Teev feed.

Thankfully, Bay was more interested in eating than in what she was doing. With a few hand motions, she started a search on the cropped image of the building showing through the window in her second drawing. She also checked the items on the tables in front of the white-dressed workers. They were definitely not packing readymeals. Too bad she couldn't show Bay the sketch.

With a sigh, she pushed the iTeev up on her head and dug into her readymeal.

The Teev cameras around the building were on alert for Grogovit, so Reese and Bay weren't overly concerned about watching for him, but after two hours, a flood of employees left the building, and Reese started studying those who passed. She pulled her iTeev back over her eyes to watch them through the darkened windows of the shuttle. Tiny CivID notifications popped up on her holoscreen next to their images. No Grogovit.

She sighed again and checked on her database search. Nothing. Still no luck identifying the building in the window.

"You never do like waiting," Bay said with a laugh.

"Who does?"

"I can think of a lot worse things to be doing. Anyway, we might as well read up on him while we wait." He activated the shuttle's onboard Teev and brought up everything the enforcer database had on Grogovit.

"Good idea." Reese removed her iTeev, folded it into a square, and clipped it back into the holder on her left sleeve. Then she studied the information as Bay's fingers swiped through images on the holoscreen that hovered over the low dashboard.

"He's apparently a huge advocate of the colonies," Bay said.

"Of course he is. That's three hundred thousand captive customers. Even if they're not paying, someone is." Reese couldn't keep the bitterness from her voice.

Bay lifted his gaze to stare at her, his dark eyes curious. "You say stuff like that sometimes, as if you know something about the colonies. I thought you were never stationed in one."

She hadn't shared details of her origins, and as far as she knew, he didn't have clearance to look at her personnel file. "I don't know anything," she said. "But construction on the colonies was started shortly after Breakdown, so they've been there for, what, seventy years? I just think that maybe the children aren't like the parents who were originally put there because they couldn't or wouldn't work to support themselves. That's all."

"Well, they should be integrated with society soon," Bay said placatingly. "It's not like they'll be giving them many birth orders, right? Not when so many responsible people are waiting."

"Yeah, maybe." There had always seemed to be a lot of children in Colony 6 when she'd been there. Of course, that was twenty years ago. Who knew what was going on there now?

More time passed as they read about Grogovit. "Look at that." Bay brought up an image of a woman about Reese's age. Her belly was extended with advanced pregnancy, and she was also holding a toddler's hand. "He's what, about three? And she's already pregnant again."

"That's Grogovit's wife?" Reese had seen the woman in earlier images, but she looked different in this picture.

"Yeah. Her face is retaining water. They do that, you know." A hint of anger entered his tone. "They've only been married five years. Letisha and I applied every nine months for ten years before we got even one acceptance." What he didn't say was that despite claims to the contrary, money and position did have some bearing on who was awarded the birth orders.

Reese studied the image on the holoscreen. The raven-haired woman was much younger than her husband. Nearly twenty-one years, to be exact, but with many people living well into their one hundred and twenty-fifth years, that wasn't unusual. In order to maintain the current two million citizens and preserve the scarce resources available after Breakdown, only one birth order was issued for every recorded death. The orders were awarded every three months, with a six-month waiting period between applications, which ironically meant people could apply every nine months. Presumably everyone in the CORE should be able to have one child, and couples two children, but with people living longer, most had to wait years longer than expected before it was their turn, and then they were often allowed only one birth. Any genetic defect in the potential parents' genes eliminated them completely.

Bay closed the holo display with an impatient downward motion. "Maybe we ought to go inside and see if he's still there. If he is, there should be one secretary or night watchman or something holding down the place until he leaves."

Reese blew out a frustrated sigh. "I guess so. At least we can ask if anyone's seen him."

Bay frowned. "He might have already left, but incognito."

Reese stared at him as something clicked into place, something that made her feel stupid. "You mean since the guy is involved in drugs, he wouldn't be above illegally masking his CivID when he left the building?"

"He might be worried enough to go check on his operation. Or even to move it."

"If you're right, he could have left hours ago." Reese slapped her door in an impatient gesture. "There's no way we'll find him."

Bay nodded his big head regretfully. "Let's go in and ask if he's still in. Better than staying out here all night while he's somewhere else."

Reese's excitement drained away. So much for following the man and taking him by surprise.

She pushed her door open. "Fine. Let's go."

CHAPTER 4

The building's front double doors weren't locked, but it was apparent the regular office hours had ended. A large mechanical cleaner, a boxy affair with gently rounded edges, ambled across the open space, followed by a chubby man with hands thrust into the pockets of his gray outfit.

The receptionist behind the ornate metal desk stood and began speaking before looking up. "I'm sorry we're—" She broke off as she caught sight of their uniforms, her face going slack with surprise. "Oh." It was more a gasp than a word.

Her name was Belfora, according to her nametag. She was young, probably only a year or two out of a certificate institute. Her black hair was pulled up on top of her head in an elaborate elevated twist. Her eyes were outlined meticulously in thick black, followed by blue glitter eye shadow that reached up to her lacquered brows and ended in a sweeping curl of blue near her temples. Her mouth was outlined in the same blue. The elaborate face paint was a recent craze among the well-to-do younger generation, but with CORE-required updates on all current "looks" for the database, most of the population couldn't be bothered. A yearly update was pain enough.

"Is Mr. Grogovit still in his office?" Bay said casually.

Belfora blinked, recovering her voice and a bit of attitude. "I believe he's gone home. He usually does before five. Unless . . . do you have an appointment?"

"Answer the question." Reese jabbed a finger at the woman's iTeev lying on the counter. "Or would you like to check our credentials?"

Belfora let out a barely masked sigh. "Almost everyone has gone home, even those who come in after lunch." She stared at them pointedly, as if to imply that they were holding her up from leaving as well. When they didn't react, she reluctantly brought up a holoscreen and typed a few commands. Within seconds, she shook her head. "His iTeev must be turned off, and he's not answering his office Teev. Like I said before, it looks like he's gone home."

Reese exchanged a glance with her partner. It wasn't overly unusual that Grogovit had turned off his iTeev, though most people in the CORE never did. Reese powered hers down when she wanted to be sure she was alone. Because more than once she'd seen the division's Teev Aided Dispatch Alert System, or the TAD-Alert, activate an iTeev without the owner's permission. Yes, it had been in an emergency situation, but the very fact that it had happened made Reese nervous. Naturally, a rich pus bag like Grogovit could be as paranoid as she was, especially given his side business.

"Thank you. We'll try him at home," Bay said.

Reese followed him away from the desk, dragging her feet. She doubted Grogovit was at home, not when an advocate just happened to show up to help one of his employees. Grogovit would have been informed, and she knew from her sketches that he was heads deep in this—or at least Cruz believed he was. But if she didn't find Grogovit and track his path tonight, it might be too late to get anything solid on him.

"There are likely ways out of the building that aren't covered by camera," Reese said as Bay turned to see why she wasn't catching up with him. "So the cameras not seeing him leave don't mean all that much. It's not as if this is public property. And once he's inside a vehicle, the Teev might not be able to read his CivID."

Bay made a face. "True. But if I was leaving to check on my nefarious activities, I certainly wouldn't leave a trail. And I'd come back here and leave publicly to give myself a good alibi."

"Which he doesn't have now because he's not here."

"Or he's here and just not answering. Maybe he's taking a dump."

Reese frowned. Bay might be right, but unless cameras eventually did record Grogovit leaving the building, they'd have at least one more reason to question him.

For a moment neither spoke. They stood watching as the chubby janitor walking near the boxy cleaner reached out and touched some controls on the waist-high surface, most likely redirecting it to a spot for additional cleaning. Reese knew from experience that the man wasn't really needed for general cleaning, but it was a way that the few mentally deficient people in the CORE could earn a living. Which was why the term "walking with the cleaners" was both a reference to a mental condition and as a comment on a person's intelligence.

"Let's send the receptionist up to physically check if he's there," Reese said.

They turned back to the desk, where the receptionist was still standing, her painted eyes alert. The glitter seemed to shine. "Is there something else?"

"Belfora, we'd like you to check if Mr. Grogovit is in his office," Reese told her.

Belfora's lacquered brows drew together, causing a deep groove between them. "He's not or he'd answer."

"Please check." Reese held the younger woman's eyes until she finally turned back to her Teev display. After manipulating a few controls, she said, "Hi Ceecia. Can you check Mr. Grogovit's office to see if he's left? Some enfo—someone wants to see him."

The voice answered, but it was low enough that Reese didn't catch it.

The receptionist looked at Reese. "Sorry. My colleague verified that she saw him leave three hours ago. I'm sure you'll find him at home. Shall I call there for you?"

"No," Reese said quickly. If Grogovit was there, they might still have the option of following him. At the very least, she wanted to surprise the man.

Reese was about to leave when another idea came to her, a long shot at best, but it couldn't hurt to ask Belfora if she recognized the building that was visible through the window in her second drawing of Grogovit. Depending on how long she'd been with the company and what her jobs had been, she might know something.

"I have another question," Reese said. "I'm going to show you a holo of a building. Tell me if you've seen it before."

"Okay, sure." Belfora said easily enough, but her face was tight, and it made Reese wonder what kind of boss Grogovit was. Cruz had been so frightened of him that he'd confessed to manufacturing drugs. But the receptionist's attitude seemed to come from genuine loyalty.

Reese put on her iTeev and pulled up her second drawing. She blurred Grogovit's face and the objects on the tables, but left the workers and the building framed by the window. "Okay, I'm going to broadcast something to your iTeev and see if you recognize it."

But Belfora was in the mood to show off. She pushed a

few keys on her holo keyboard and the wall behind her came alive with Reese's drawing. It was impressive, even if Reese saw larger-than-life screens every day at division. Holo emitters required to create this large of a display weren't available in most households, and the company having access to the technology was a sign of their prosperity.

Bay looked up at the image and then back at Reese, a question in his eyes that she pretended not to see. "I got this from an informant a few weeks back." This was more for Bay's benefit than the receptionist's. "We believe the building in the foreground might be owned by Kordell Corp. What I want to know is if you recognize either it or the outside building that is framed by the window. Look closely now and think before you decide."

Reese watched Belfora carefully as the younger woman studied the image, but there was no sign of recognition as she finally turned back to them, shaking her head. "Sorry. I've only worked here a couple years, and only recently was transferred to the main office. But those workers are dressed like ours, so it could be one of our warehouses."

"I know!" The voice came from behind Reese, so close that she almost jumped. She turned to see the janitor standing behind her, his rounded face staring up at the huge screen.

"You've seen this place?" Bay asked him, doubt dripping from his words.

"I see," the man said. His face still pointed toward the screen, but his eyes riveted on Reese. "I see. I see all."

"Don't mind him," Belfora interjected. "He doesn't know what he's saying. He used to work for us in another department, but there were some problems."

"What problems?" Reese asked.

"I see. I see!" The janitor's eyes rolled back to the holoscreen.

Belfora shrugged, so Reese pushed her for more. "You can tell us here or down at division."

Belfora scowled. "You know, financial problems."

"Embezzling?"

"Yeah." Belfora raised her voice to continue because the janitor was mumbling something else now, louder than before. "He was an accountant and was caught stealing. Several times, in fact. He was convicted and sentenced to enhancement." The janitor fell silent during the last sentence and her words sounded too loud in the sudden silence. She lowered her voice. "They still let him work here, only now he walks with the cleaners."

"My head." The janitor's shoulders drooped forward, but his eyes still angled up to watch Reese's face. "They fixed my head, but I still see."

Reese pushed her iTeev up, exposing her eyes to the janitor in an effort to connect. "You know where this building is?" she asked gently, stepping toward the man but keeping a hand on her stunner just in case.

The janitor shot a look at Belfora and then lunged at Reese. His big hands landed on her shoulder, his grip more heavy than tight. She jabbed her stunner into his side, ready to send him to the ground in agony with the close contact feature, but she hesitated when he froze in place.

"Elm and First, third building," he whispered in her ear.

Bay appeared behind the janitor, ready to drag him away from Reese, but she shook her head. A sketch filled her vision. An image of a three-story building.

"Elm and First?" she whispered back at the janitor. "You sure?"

"Third building. Don't tell!" the man staggered sideways a few feet, then whirled in a surprisingly dexterous move and lumbered back to the still-working cleaner, talking to himself, his shoulders hunched as if expecting a beating.

"Did he hurt you?" Bay asked, his brow furrowed.

"No. He's harmless." Reese pulled her iTeev back over her eyes, fighting the itch to record the sketch from the janitor's mind.

"What did he say to you?" Belfora asked.

"Nothing intelligible," Reese said. "Thank you for your time. We'll stop by Mr. Grogovit's place and talk to his wife. Or come back tomorrow."

"I'll let him know you were here then."

"No need." Reese started for the door, her gaze sliding toward the janitor, who was hunched over his cleaner. Once again, his eyes were angled toward her, but he didn't appear to see anything. Was he crazy? Or was the building she'd seen in his mind important?

She waited until she was outside to look up Elm and First Street on her iTeev. The instant the juncture appeared on her holoscreen, she knew it was the same building she'd seen in the sketch from the janitor. Her fingers still itched to draw it.

"Put on your iTeev," she said to Bay. "I want to show you something."

Her partner did as she requested, and she broadcasted the building to him. "This is the address the janitor whispered in my ear. I'm thinking we need to check to see if Kordell Corp owns the building."

"But why didn't you tell me you had an informant related to our bust?"

Reese shrugged. "It didn't seem to mean anything at the time. Nothing identifiable. I just asked them about it on a whim."

"Fine. Don't tell me who your source is. I'm okay with that. I don't tell you all mine either, but let's go check out the building. I want to nail this pus bag."

"I agree." Reese led the way to their shuttle.

On the way to the location, she drew the sketch from the

janitor's mind, and if Bay wondered why she chose to draw the building she'd looked up on her iTeev, he didn't ask.

"I only hope if there are drugs at the building," he said, "that we also find something that links Grogovit to the operation."

Reese hoped so too.

CHAPTER 5

At first glance, the building looked deserted, but closer examination revealed a faint glow behind the window coverings, as if someone had left an interior light on, perhaps by mistake. Or maybe they were nightlights that came on automatically. But there seemed to be nothing else that indicated human presence.

"What do you think?" Bay asked.

Reese checked the data on her iTeev. "Forty-five people have entered in the past two hours, but none of them was Grogovit."

"Why go to work so late?" Bay wondered aloud.

"To do nothing good, I'm guessing."

One of the perks of living in the CORE, at least according to the Elite, was the six-hour workday. While some people liked to work those hours in the afternoon, a night shift was nearly unheard of outside law enforcement and the colonies.

"Let's go in," Reese said. She punched a command on her iTeev and brought up the universal enforcer code that would allow them access to the building. She broadcast the code into the handprint reader locking the door. Nothing. The only way that could happen was if the door had been programed to ignore enforcer override.

Reese frowned. "Let's go around back. Schematics say there's a second entrance. Maybe the code will work there."

They went down the alleyway next to the building, found a gate, and climbed over it. Reese spied a private camera on the building, one that must be linked to Kordell's private security and not the Teev feed. She activated a camera disruptor on her suit, which would interrupt the recording. Whoever was in the building, she didn't want them warned.

The override didn't work at the back door either. Something was definitely off.

"Now what?" Reese asked. "There doesn't seem to be a way to alert anyone inside." She banged on the door for emphasis.

Bay made a fist, looking ready to help her break down the door through sheer force. But almost instantly he sighed and relaxed. "Now we wait." He touched the iTeev on his sleeve, swiping a few screens. "At least a dozen people entered the building six hours ago. Whatever they're doing here, I doubt people are working longer than that. Which means one of them is bound to go home soon. Or maybe someone will come out to see why their cameras aren't working."

They waited, one on either side of the door. In only six minutes, a much shorter time than Reese expected, the door opened, a slash of bright light nearly blinding them. As a man stepped through the door, he glanced casually at Reese before doing a double take at her uniform. Color bled from his face. Nodding at Reese, he put his head down, moving forward quickly.

But Bay was already standing in his path. "Sorry buddy," Bay said, pointing his stunner at the man's throat. "It's not quitting time yet."

Reese stopped the sliding door from closing with her boot and peeked into the brightly lit hallway. The door obediently slid back open. No other employees were in sight, but she couldn't count on it staying that way. "I'm going in," Reese said, stepping through. She stopped the door from closing again with the manual override on the wall.

Bay nodded. "Right behind you. Just going to take care of this guy."

"What are you going to do with me?" Panic spilled into the man's voice.

"Shut up. You'll live to go to jail." Bay snapped cuffs over the man's wrists and shoved him into the building.

That was all Reese saw as she sprinted down the hallway. The bright lights alone would have told her something was wrong, if she didn't already guess. This was a building ready for business, a business someone wanted hidden from the outside world.

She didn't see cameras in the hallway, and that surprised her, but maybe they were confident in their security. Another corridor intersected hers, and she veered left, following a faint humming sound. She nearly blundered into someone, catching the sound of voices almost too late. She threw herself against a door in the hallway, pulling at the knob, grateful there was no handprint reader. The door gave under her weight. Leaving the door open, she crouched inside the room and watched two people pass her location. They were both dressed in white from head to toe, and their voices were weary. Reese couldn't tell if they were men or women, but they could have been any workers at any factory. She felt a momentary concern that maybe her drawing had led her astray. Maybe this building was simply another readymeal packaging plant.

No. Her sketches always portrayed whatever a witness believed he'd seen. And this afternoon her witness had been willing to incriminate himself rather than spill what he knew about Grogovit.

Looking around, Reese realized the room she'd ducked into was an employee breakroom, complete with readymeal dispensers and lounging areas. The accommodations looked as good as those offered by her enforcer division, so obviously Grogovit wanted to keep his employees happy. Was that why they were willing to make juke for him? She didn't believe it for a minute. Money had to be their motive for betraying the CORE. Then remembering Cruz's fear, Reese wondered if maybe there was more to it than that.

When the voices faded, she emerged silently from the room. Where was her partner? He couldn't be all that far behind with only the one man to stash somewhere. Unless he'd run into additional trouble.

Heads up, she texted to him on her iTeev. *Two workers coming your way.*

The humming was louder now, and when she came to a set of double doors, she peeked into the glass window at the top, unsurprised to see the spacious factory room from Cruz's second sketch—or the scene was so similar that she couldn't tell them apart. Two long rows of white-dressed employees, their backs toward each other across a short aisle, stood working in front of tables. Behind those tables sat three-meter-tall, oblong machines that were wider than three police shuttles, end-to-end. Above each of the machines, dozens of tubes snaked down from the ceiling, like umbilical cords, disappearing into different areas of the metal surface. Likely a steady supply of drug ingredients, if she had to bet.

There were roughly twenty-four tables and machines in each of those two long rows, so whatever the setup in the rest of the building, there was work for at least forty-eight employees in just this room, or probably quadruple that if they ran four six-hour shifts. Which meant more juke than Reese had imagined was being manufactured here.

Checking to make sure her suit camera was on, Reese debated what to do. There was enough light in the room that the people working at the tables would see her immediately if she entered here. No way could she make it past them to hide behind the machines. She thought fleetingly of disguising herself as a worker, but giving up the safety of her suit wasn't an option. She needed to find another entrance into the large room.

She continued down the hall, checking the few doors that appeared. She had her stunner in her dominant left hand now, but her right was close to the nine mil. She didn't want to hurt the employees, but she fully intended to stop anyone who tried to prevent her from getting the proof she needed.

Finally, she opened a door to an office that was not much larger than her own tiny quarters back at division. The aroma of peanuts wafted out at her. The lights were on in the room and a Teev holoscreen hovered over the desk as if awaiting its owner. More important, however, was the door and shuttered window on the far side. If her sense of direction had it right, that should open up onto the factory floor.

The aroma of peanuts intensified as she stepped inside the office. It wasn't the smell of the real peanut paste served at fancy restaurants in town, but the stronger, cloying, oily stench of the synthetic version used in readymeals. A surge of anticipation spread through her. The factory might have at one time processed actual readymeals, but far more certain was the fact that in forty-five of the last sixty juke hypos they'd confiscated from students, synthetic peanut paste had made up part of the drug's delivery system.

In a few steps she reached the door on the other side of the room, easing it open far enough to peek out. The humming grew louder, but not unpleasantly so, as if the equipment was well maintained. As it had to be. Each finished drug hypo would be good for a couple of hits. If the contents weren't mixed correctly, the user would die sooner rather than later, which would hurt their bottom line.

The door opened behind the machinery, where the light was dimmer, and where it was unlikely that the employees, intent on their work, would notice her. Unless she called undue attention to herself. She emerged, moving slowly to the back of the closest machine.

The smell of peanuts was less prominent in the larger room but still cloying. Her stomach tightened at the stench, and she began breathing through her mouth. She eased around the back and up the side of the machine until she could glimpse the worker on the next machine over. Methodically, the man used a sensor to check something on the hypos from his table before setting them into a slotted conveyer belt that fed into the machine. At the same time, boxed hypos, presumably ones the worker put in earlier, spat out on a higher belt, the boxes dropping into a huge cart next to the machine.

According to the sketch from Crew's mind, Grogovit had been here at least once, but that was no guarantee he had come here tonight. There were plenty of places people could hide if they went off grid, especially when they had underground connections. If Grogovit wasn't somewhere in the building, Reese wouldn't have a solid case against him, but she would at least shut down this factory, which would mean hundreds of thousands of hypos off the market. Fewer addicts would jump off buildings, attack their families or coworkers, or burn down homes. The long-term effect of continuous juke use was almost always death, but it rarely happened without hurting innocents along the way.

She'd have to be satisfied with closing this factory and calling in backup, even if it meant not nailing Grogovit.

Reese had barely started to retrace her steps down the length of the machine when a movement on the far row of workers drew her attention. She drew in a sharp breath as she recognized Grogovit towering over a white-dressed man who waved his arms excitedly as he spoke. Grogovit shook his head in response, his jowly face flushed red from the tips of his large ears to his wide chin. The smaller white-dressed man hunched his shoulders, making himself appear even shorter, but that indication of subservience didn't halt his speech.

Reese pressed herself against the side of the machine behind her. Vibrations spread through her body, seeming to whisper ominously. Her heart beat furiously. Grogovit was here. She'd gambled and won. Now she had to make sure he didn't get away.

Grogovit and his companion had already moved from her sight, heading down the aisle between the rows of workers. She had to catch up with them! Then she'd call in backup.

She did pause long enough to text Bay: *Eyes on G in the big factory room. You coming?*

Making sure no one was looking in her direction, she moved easily to the next machine, where she crouched for a few seconds before moving to the next, moving quickly with the idea of working her way past Grogovit and somehow circling around him. She caught sight of him again after three rows of machines, and after four more, she was sure she was ahead. When she reached the last machine in the twelfth row, the lack of vibration told her it wasn't operational.

Keeping close against the machine, she glided along it to the front end. In the wall to her right, she could see a black-draped window. Behind that drape, she knew she'd find the view of the building she'd drawn, the one the janitor at Kordell Corp had identified to send her here. Opposite her position, near the other machine at the end of the row, she spied a set of double doors, and she wondered if that was where Grogovit was headed. That machine was operational, but the worker who manned it bent intently over his table, his back toward her, and she was confident that with Grogovit nearby, he wouldn't turn in her direction.

She crouched near the table at the front and contemplated stepping out behind Grogovit as he passed, but his shoes stopped at the edge of the table. She risked a peek and spied Grogovit and his shorter companion standing with their backs toward her, with Grogovit almost close enough to reach under the table and touch his leg. A large, flat-faced man also stood several paces to Grogovit's side, partway into the aisle between the rows of machines. Unlike Grogovit, he was pure muscle.

Bodyguard, Reese decided.

She could hear their conversation now, and she suspected they had chosen this location near the end of the room precisely because of the relative privacy and lower volume of noise. From how close they were to the nonworking machine, she was sure the worker opposite them couldn't hear them. The man did look once over his shoulder at the group across the aisle before studiously bending over his work.

"Will they come here?" asked the short man, sounding anxious.

"No. I already told you—it's taken care of." Grogovit's gruff voice held impatience. "That's why I was late getting here tonight. I had my people set up just enough evidence to point to Cruz—and only to Cruz. Tomorrow the advocate will let him give the enforcers the location. It will look like a one-man operation."

"You sure they're going to buy that? We're the only supplier for the city. A small operation would only be able to supply a tiny percentage with our special mix."

Grogovit snorted. "It doesn't matter what they think they

might know. Cruz won't say anything except what the advocate tells him. He'll protect his family. You just keep production running smoothly here." That statement told Reese the shorter man was the manager of this factory, or at least one of them.

"Right, right." The manager fiddled with his white plastic hair covering, glancing nervously at the back of the employee across the aisle.

"I do want you to be on the lookout," Grogovit added. "Just to make sure. If you see anything out of the ordinary, alert me on the secure channel."

"Okay boss. I'll keep an eye on things."

"Good. And remind everyone about keeping their mouths shut. Make sure the other distributors don't mess up like Cruz did. I won't stand for it."

"Of course. Of course." The way the manager spoke told Reese he had already reassured Grogovit various times. But Grogovit hadn't gotten where he was now by being easily reassured. No, Reese was sure he'd be careful.

Time was running out. If Reese didn't act soon, she would lose the opportunity to take Grogovit red-handed. But where was her partner? She wasn't worried about the employees' interference when she took down Grogovit. With her weapons, they wouldn't be much of a challenge, even if they stuck around instead of fleeing. She'd use the temper laser on them, which would make them compliable to her suggestions.

But she did worry about the bodyguard. He looked like he might have enforcer training, and with her luck, he'd probably be among the one percent of the population who was immune to a temper laser. He was also likely armed, despite the CORE ban on civilian weapons. Guns turned up regularly enough from the underground for her not to discount the possibility.

Bay, where are you? she thought.

She typed out a hurried request for additional backup from

division before realizing with a sinking feeling that none of her messages to Bay had actually sent. Something in this room had to be blocking her iTeev connection. Which meant Bay had no idea she'd found Grogovit or might need backup.

"Okay then, I'm off," Grogovit said, tilting his head toward the doors nearest them.

Making an instant decision, Reese sprang from her hiding place and stepped out behind the men, pointing her stunner at them. "Stop," she ordered. "Tadum Grogovit, you are under arrest for suspected drug manufacture and distribution."

The manager gasped as he whirled to face her, but Grogovit turned without hurry, regarding her complacently, perhaps even with a bit of amusement.

"Please step away from Mr. Grogovit," Reese told the manager.

To her surprise, the manager didn't obey. Instead, he launched himself at her. She side-stepped him and arced her elbow down on his back, slamming him to the ground, the close contact feature on her stunner finishing the job.

She'd been quick, but not quick enough. As she righted herself, Grogovit's bodyguard was at her side, a gun pointed at her head, the only part of her not protected by her suit. Her heart beat furiously in her chest, and every one of her senses seemed acute. The smell of peanuts was suddenly overwhelming, her breathing too loud, and the sweat beading on her brow felt like a flood. Her mind was also clear. They couldn't afford to let her go, and that meant she was excess baggage. Or maybe one more corpse that would be found in the river. But they'd ask her questions first, if only to make sure she was alone. There was still time. A few minutes.

"I think it's you who should put down that stunner," Grogovit said with an arrogant smirk. "It's no match for—"

Reese fired from her hip with her right hand, and the

bodyguard jerked as her bullet slammed between his chest and right shoulder. He grunted with pain as his gun crashed to the floor. Reese pointed her nine mil at Grogovit and her stunner at the bodyguard, who clutched at his wound. Blood seeped through his fingers.

Reese smiled mockingly. They never looked at her other hand. They always assumed there was only one danger. Still, if Bay had been around, he would bawl her out for taking the shot. So much could have gone wrong.

But it hadn't. Not this time.

"You were saying?" she said to Grogovit.

His complacency vanished, a flush of anger taking its place. The vast room had gone still during their confrontation, but now employees ran in a disorganized flurry to the far door, casting fearful backwards glances at her and Grogovit.

Grogovit didn't try to stop them.

The bodyguard, perhaps thinking her distracted, gathered his energy and lunged at her. She kicked out to keep him away and let the contacts on the stunner fly, piercing his skin. Convulsing with the electric shock, he fell to the ground.

A sketch flashed into her mind—from Grogovit, she thought—the image of a dark-haired woman. Could it be his wife? She couldn't see the woman's face, only her long, slender, naked back.

Grogovit took the opportunity to run. But Reese was ready. She wanted to fire, to eliminate this slut munching whore wrangler, but that would be letting him off too easy. No, he was going down.

Holstering her stunner, she jumped toward him, slamming her left fist into the side of his neck. The effort hurt her hand, but it had the desired effect. He gagged and started coughing.

"Next time, it's a bullet," she growled. "Now get down on the ground so I can cuff you."

With a glare, Grogovit complied. "I can pay you," he said. "Anything you want. More than you'll make in ten years."

She finished the cuffs and sneered into his face. "What I want is you out of business. Just shut up."

Reese took his iTeev and made him give her access. No surprise that his device worked. Apparently trust of his employees didn't go as far as allowing Teev connections on the premises without a special code. She immediately called division for backup. That completed, her mind was free to worry about Bay. Something terrible must have happened to him.

But even as the thought came to her mind, he burst through the double doors leading into the factory floor. His hair was disheveled and he was breathing hard.

"Reese," he called, sprinting toward her.

Relief seeped through her, but she masked it by giving a warning kick to the bodyguard who was already stirring on the floor. "Stay still or I'll put the bullet in your heart this time."

She gave Bay a once-over as he reached her. Besides a cut on his forehead, he didn't look too bad. "It took you long enough," she growled. Gesturing to the kneeling Grogovit, she added, "You missed all the fun."

"Oh, I found plenty." He leaned over and cuffed the sprawled bodyguard. "Ran into two like these. Plus, all the employees started leaving. I was only able to detain nine of them. I had to blast them with a temper and lock them in the employee lounge."

Reese groaned. "Don't tell me you welded the door shut." He'd done that once as a rookie and had talked about it ever since.

"Hey, why not? It's a tried and proven method. At least we know they're not going anywhere. We got witnesses. That should make you happy."

He was right. She wanted as many witnesses as possible,

though there should be enough drugs in the room to send Grogovit to a colony—or worse.

"You don't have anything on me," Grogovit said into the lull of conversation, his sneer changing his face into a hideous mask. "I own this building, but I have no idea what they're doing here."

Reese laughed. "I have a recording that says differently."

He paled. "You can't do that."

"Oh, yes, I can," she said without expression. "This is the CORE. Not some weak pre-Breakdown society. We won't allow you to tear down what we've built."

Grogovit hadn't been born in the colonies. He couldn't possibly imagine how good it was out here compared to inside, and even if she was sometimes uncertain about the CORE's methods, the Elite had created peace after the horrible chaos of Breakdown. They had protected the weak and the sick, and even the lazy. All Grogovit and his ilk did was bite the hand that fed them.

Two more enforcers appeared at the far end of the room. "Looks like our backup's here," she said.

Bay reached down and hauled Grogovit to his feet. "I'm going to enjoy this," he said. "Every last bit."

"You can say that again," Reese returned with a grin.

And he did.

CHAPTER 6

Two days later, on Thursday, the Controller's office convened a hearing under the direction of the Director, leader of the CORE. The Controller's office was over all enforcers and was responsible for making sure people kept the law, but only the Director's office could pronounce final sentence on the most severe cases. With Kordell Corp being as powerful as it was, Reese knew from the beginning that the Director's office would be involved in Grogovit's sentencing.

The Director wouldn't be conducting the proceedings herself, of course, but her Magistrate Assistant would be present as her representative and would pass sentencing. Reese and Bay were called to be in attendance, though they weren't needed as witnesses since Reese's suit camera and the evidence at the scene was deemed to be more than enough for the Magistrate to make her decision.

The cavernous, circular hearing room located in New York's main administration building smelled of antiseptic, as though someone had scrubbed the burgundy walls, the shiny black tile floors, and the circle of ebony columns ringing the room in preparation for a medical operation. In front of the Magistrate's raised dais, upon which perched an impressive wooden desk, sat a U-shaped row of a dozen chairs. Only half of them were occupied. Grogovit and his advocate—not the same advocate who had come to speak for Cruz—were on the right edge of the chairs, close to the Magistrate's left side. Next to them were two uniformed enforcers Reese didn't know, an unfamiliar man dressed in a green medical jacket, and a tech guy named Zeka from her division.

The room was lit only in the middle by several large spotlights, and though proceedings were by invitation only, Reese felt an uncanny sensation of being observed from the shadows at the edges of the room, perhaps by someone peering from behind the columns.

Grogovit stared at them as they passed him, his sneer apparent on his fleshy mouth, but Reese ignored his stare and headed for the chairs on the opposite side of the U.

They were barely seated when a disembodied female voice called out in a measured, slightly mechanical tone, "All rise for the Magistrate."

They came to their feet and watched as a black-robed figure appeared out of nowhere and strode onto the dais. It was only then Reese understood that the dais and the desk and the Magistrate herself were being projected via holoscreen. The Magistrate settled in the tall-backed chair behind the desk, looking every bit as real to Reese as Grogovit.

"Please be seated," announced the disembodied voice. "The proceedings are now in progress."

"Is it just me," Bay whispered to Reese as they settled in their seats, "or does Grogovit look a little too cocky?"

An unidentifiable fear prickled through Reese's body. "Maybe."

"And his advocate too. He looks like a rooster with that wave of hair slicked back on his head. I wonder if he filed the appropriate forms to dye it that bright red. I've half a mind to check so we can arrest him."

"Shh," she said. "The Magistrate's looking this way."

Or she appeared to be. It was difficult to tell the exact direction of her gaze under the black mask that protected her identity. No one knew her real name except the Director and the three heads of CORE government, and possibly a handful of chosen Elite. It was a system designed to carry out justice swiftly while still allowing the Magistrate to pursue a personal life. For all Reese knew, maybe she wasn't even female. Her collar-length hair was slicked to her head in a non-identifying manner, and she appeared tall enough to be either sex under the heavy-looking robes.

How did Grogovit feel not being permitted to see the face of his judge and jury? Reese studied him for any sign of reaction and had to admit he didn't seem worried.

Once they were seated, a full minute passed and no one moved. Then, as if by some unseen signal, the Magistrate began talking, her voice husky and casual, but full of power.

"Tadum Grogovit, you are accused of manufacturing juke and distributing to the detriment of the CORE. What do you have to say in your defense?"

The advocate arose and started to speak, but the Magistrate waved him to silence. "I asked Mr. Grogovit."

Grogovit came to his feet, bowing slightly before speaking. "I own the building in question, Magistrate," he said, his voice placating and softly pleading, a tone Reese was sure he'd practiced for the past two days. "Or rather, I'm part owner since the building belongs to Kordell Corp. We have multiple holdings and are responsible for nearly all of the readymeal packaging in the CORE."

"I am aware of your company's reputation," the Magistrate said without intonation. "I want to know why you were manufacturing juke on the premises."

Grogovit gulped audibly, and when he continued, his voice had lost some of its confidence. "After I heard that an employee of mine had confessed to running juke, I was in the process of doing an onsite inspection of all our buildings to make sure our business wasn't compromised in any way. I was as surprised as anyone with what I found."

There was a momentary lull, in which the advocate said, "May I speak?"

The Magistrate shifted her head slightly and nodded.

The advocate bowed, and the red wave on his head tilted dangerously. "The manager of the building has confessed to setting up the drug operation. And every employee we've talked to so far has denied that Mr. Grogovit had knowledge that his building was being used for such a despicable venture."

Shock reverberated through Reese, and she exchanged an uneasy glance with Bay. Grogovit had assured them he'd get off, but could he really convince so many people to lie for him? Surely under questioning, they would break. A shot or two with the mood-altering temper laser would make them pliable, and there were stronger drugs to get to the truth, if authorized.

"I understand the manager committed suicide last night," the Magistrate said.

"That's right." The advocate lowered his eyes as if saddened by the loss.

Reese felt a growing sense of disbelief. The manager was dead?

"What a coincidence," Bay whispered grimly.

The Magistrate looked down at the desk in front of her for a moment, studying something not visible to her audience. "I was also informed that all of the nine detained employees and three guards have come down with a fever that renders them incapable of coherent speech."

The advocate nodded firmly. "We believe it was due to a bad batch of their drugs, which is poetic justice, if you care to look at it that way. Most of them should survive, in time."

"I see. That will be all. You and your client may sit." The Magistrate gazed in the general direction of the green-robed man. "Doctor, I assume you have the employees under your care?"

The man arose, nodding vigorously. "I do. It's nothing like I've ever seen before, though. I'm not sure any of them will make it, but I'll know more about their prognosis within the next few days."

"Thank you."

The doctor nodded and settled again in his seat.

Reese wanted to leap up and protest. Could the Magistrate see what was going on here, or was she completely taken by Grogovit's lies?

For a time, a tense silence filled the room, and then the Magistrate said, "I also understand there is a visual and sound recording of the arrest," she said finally. "I would like to see that now."

The tech guy arose. "I'm Hap Zeka, representing the New York Enforcer Division. I had planned to show that here," he said, casting an apologetic glance in Reese's direction, "but I learned just before this meeting that the feed has been compromised."

The Magistrate's back stiffened. "How?" The single frigid word seemed to reach inside Reese's brain with the force of a command.

Hap's shoulders lifted in a shrug. "At this point we're not sure. It was fine when I first got it and then when I tried to cue it up today, the sound was gone and the images were distorted.

My whole team can testify that no one messed with it. We simply don't know what happened."

"But you saw what was on the file?"

Hap shook his head. "Only part of it. The beginning."

"Will you be able to recover the recording?"

"Perhaps. We're working on that now."

"How long do you need?"

"A day. Maybe two."

"Very well. I will expect to see it on Saturday morning, so let's get it done." She paused a heartbeat before adding to the still-standing Zeka. "You may sit."

Now the Magistrate's face shifted in Reese's direction, the dark eyes glittering briefly through the holes in the mask as they caught the light in the room where the Magistrate's body actually sat. "Detective Reese Parker?"

Reese stood. "I'm Detective Parker." She could feel Bay beside her, and despite the intense focus of the Magistrate, she glanced at him, grateful for his support.

"I understand you were an eye witness?" the Magistrate asked.

"Magistrate," the advocate protested, jumping to his feet, "this is highly unusual. Historically, only proper enforcer surveillance is admitted in these types of proceedings." By type, he had to mean when medical enhancement was likely to be the result of a guilty verdict. Reese wondered if that meant Grogovit wasn't as confident as he looked.

The Magistrate, her mask barely tilting in his direction, waved a hand, as if flicking away his comment. "Nevertheless, I will hear what the detective has to say."

"But we were not aware that Detective Parker would be a witness. We are not prepared with her background information, and under CORE law, we are permitted to request a delay."

This time the Magistrate looked at him for a full three seconds without response. Finally, she spoke. "Very well, but I do want to determine if she will be able to testify in these proceedings." Not waiting until he was fully seated, her head swiveled back to Reese. "Did you witness the events personally? Please tell me briefly how you came to be at the location."

"I witnessed everything my suit camera did," Reese told her. "As to how we got there, we went to Mr. Grogovit's office and the information there led us to the factory where we arrested him. I must add that it might be significant the Teev feed has no record of Mr. Grogovit leaving his office or arriving at the factory."

The Magistrate asked, "Are you suggesting that he was masking his CivID?"

Reese wanted to agree, but next to her Bay cleared his throat softly in a way that she knew meant she should think about that carefully before she spoke. He was right. She might believe Grogovit was purposefully avoiding being tracked, which was clearly against CORE law, but she didn't want to be seen as having a vendetta against him.

"I only know that for nearly half the day the Teev cameras could not track him as it did the other employees."

The Magistrate nodded. "Very well. I will take that into account. I want you prepared to testify on Saturday morning. I know it isn't usual procedure, but I'm not entirely confident they will recover your recording. I believe your testimony will be useful."

Reese sat down, not missing the furious stare the advocate shot at her.

The Magistrate again looked down before saying, "Detective Danvers?"

Bay hefted himself to his feet. "That's me."

"You were also at the factory. Will you be able to testify to a conversation between Mr. Grogovit and his employees?"

"No. We were separated at the factory. But we did arrest Grogovit there, and I did hear him tell us he'd get free."

Grogovit's advocate popped to his feet once again. "Because he's not guilty! Magistrate, it's clear these detectives are prejudiced against my client. I request that—"

"Sit down, advocate," the Magistrate ordered. "Do not make me ask you again."

Grogovit's advocate shut up and sank to his seat. Silence stretched out in the huge room, and Reese felt an urge to fiddle in her seat like the tech guy and his three companions. But she kept herself still. Waiting.

At last, the Magistrate spoke. "We will reconvene again on Saturday morning. I don't need to tell any of you that it's a weekend, and I'm sure we all have better things to do. I want all the evidence and witnesses present. In the meantime, Mr. Grogovit will remain in custody. You are dismissed."

"No!" Grogovit shouted, but his protest rang out on empty ears as the holoscreen depicting the Magistrate, her desk, and the dais vanished, leaving only empty space on the shiny black tile.

The enforcers stepped forward and seized Grogovit, whose head twisted as he craned to see his advocate. "You said you took care of it. You'd better fix this!"

"I did everything I could, sir," the advocate protested.

"Not yet, you haven't," snarled Grogovit. "I'm still here, aren't I?"

"Come on," said one of the enforcers, pushing him a little. "Let's go."

"Fine." Grogovit shook off his hand. "I'll go. Don't touch me."

The advocate stared after Grogovit and the enforcers in open-mouthed shock as they marched toward the exit.

"That was unexpected," Bay muttered. "I wonder how he got to your recording."

"I don't know," Reese replied grimly. "At least we got him off the streets for two more days."

Bay grinned. "You mean you did. Good job, partner. Maybe some of that glow around you will rub off and I can retire early. Letisha would like that with the baby coming."

"Not a chance in Breakdown of that. We'll both be working until your kid has a kid of his own. Unless you have a rich Elite relative in your family history that I don't know about."

He chuckled. "Well, you never know."

They started to walk past the advocate, who seemed to have fallen into some kind of trance. Bay hesitated near the man, looking as if he might say something. The advocate jerked his head to meet their gaze, his eyes haunted. "I'm a dead man. You know that, don't you?"

"Do you feel you need protection?" Reese asked him.

His stare dropped to the shiny floor that reflected the circles of light from above. "Doesn't matter what you do. I'm dead. You are too. We all are."

Reese stared at him. "Is that a threat?"

Bay tugged at her. "Don't mind him. Come Saturday, it'll be over one way or the other. And with all the mysteriously disappearing evidence, I think I know which way the Magistrate will rule, especially given your record. There's nothing more anyone can do for now." His words were matter-of-fact, but his expression was spooked.

As her partner pulled her toward the door, Reese felt the advocate's gaze digging into her all the way across the room. Firearms weren't allowed inside the chamber, so she carried only her knife inside a hidden pocket on the side of her right leg, just above her knee. Her hand went to it now. She'd bagged the biggest arrest of her life, a bigger case than most detectives landed in a lifetime. She had to believe that Zeka would repair her recording and that Grogovit would be taken care of permanently. After his enhancement, with a tiny, exact portion of his brain removed to adjust his attitude, he'd have no more will to betray his people in the CORE for personal benefit. He wouldn't hurt anyone again.

She believed that. She did. So why did she feel more afraid than when she'd lived back in Colony 6?

CHAPTER 7

Reese took off her battle helmet to let the wind rush through her hair. Driving a two-wheel scrambler was one of the best perks of her job, as only enforcers were allowed that mode of transportation. Not only could she weave in and out of the public shuttles and private cars at rush hour, but the feeling of flying through the streets of New York like this was one only a few people would ever experience.

Despite the encroaching darkness, she took the long way home, which was less crowded, even though it led her near one of the few empty zones that remained within the city borders. Two blocks of ruined buildings and destruction that had been caused by the bombs during Breakdown, and then eroded during the eighty subsequent years of neglect. Slowly, the city was reclaiming the area. This empty zone wasn't near a desolation zone, which often birthed monsters—animals changed into things of horror by nuclear fallout—so it was a hangout for local youth. Enforcers let them use it for now, but they kept a close eye on the situation. For the most part, entering the empty zone was all the rebellion the average teen was willing to risk.

Reese picked up her speed on the street that bordered the empty zone. Wind hit her face, no longer making her feel exultant, but more as if she were taking a beating.

All day she'd been thinking about her pending testimony against Grogovit. Eight of the nine sick employees and two of the guards had died during the day, and Hap Zeka had informed them this afternoon that even if he had another year, he wouldn't be able to fix her original recording. Whatever virus had attacked it, the damage was permanent. That meant the sentence the Magistrate Assistant handed down on Saturday morning would necessarily relate directly to Reese's testimony. Grogovit deserved the maximum sentence, of course, in light of the many lives he'd destroyed. How many youths had jumped to their deaths under the influence of juke, or had been sent to a welfare colony as punishment for other juke-induced crimes?

Yet Reese couldn't help thinking of the janitor at Grogovit's building. He'd once been an accountant; now, after enhancement, he walked with the cleaners. What if she was sending Grogovit to a living death?

The janitor was probably a fluke occurrence, Reese told herself. Next week or the next, Grogovit would be back in his office, his desire to break the law excised like so much waste. He'd manufacture and sell more readymeals, make love to his wife, and celebrate the birth of their second child. She had to believe that. She trusted in the CORE and all it represented.

Didn't she?

Sighing, Reese made a sharp U-turn on the deserted street. All the joy had gone from her ride, so she headed back to the apartment she rented eight blocks south of division. She wished Bay hadn't refused her invitation to meet at a restaurant like they often did on Friday nights. After their meeting with Zeka, Bay had begged off, saying Letisha wasn't feeling up to going out. With his wife's new pregnancy, it was a logical excuse, but Bay had been acting strangely all afternoon. He'd been on the phone a lot, had a meeting with Captain Homer that she hadn't been privy to, and he hadn't even accompanied her on their usual rounds, staying instead at division to file reports.

Well, Reese would go home, draw the two sketches she'd glimpsed from a couple of coworkers' minds before they drove her mad, then step under the sonic cleanser, and eat a ready-meal or two in front of the holoscreen. It wasn't as distracting as a night out, but the plan contained considerably less worry about having to see more sketches, as she invariably would in a crowd.

Unfortunately, it was also very lonely.

Despite her loneliness, pulling up to her apartment building brought a sense of contentment. She liked this place because it was relatively close to division, but far enough away from the shopping district that the area didn't see a ton of traffic. The nearest sky train stop was only minutes away on foot. These buildings were part of the few that had been built post-Breakdown, which meant they didn't have some of the comforts of the pre-Breakdown buildings—like real water showers—but they also had none of the cobbled-together repairs that were the bane of living in older buildings, repairs that invariably broke down when it was least convenient.

Most of the residents living near Reese were enforcers or workers in upscale offices. No certificate institutes were located nearby, and only one small school for younger children was within the district, so that meant less traffic. In all, it was a good place to live. Good enough that Bay, who lived in a different community, was doing his best to make sure his new apartment was somewhere near her.

Reese parked her scrambler in front of her building and had started up the small flight of stairs to the entrance when she caught a sense of motion from the corner of her left eye. She stopped and turned as something slammed into her left shoulder, knocking her backward. She hit the stairs hard. Pain spread from the shoulder, under her uniform, which could stop the penetration of a bullet at point blank range. Unfortunately, it didn't stop the pressure of impact.

She'd been shot. No doubt about it. But by whom?

The next second, they were on her. A foot lashed out viciously at her leg. Reese tried to raise her head from the stair it was on, but her body wouldn't obey. She could feel blood gushing from a split in her skull. At least some of it dribbled down the back of her neck.

"You didn't kill her, did you?" barked a guttural voice.

"Naw. Hit her in the shoulder." The second speaker was also male but had a slight nasal quality to his voice.

"You sure? She looks dead."

"She's alive," came a third voice from further away, a calm, cultured, confident voice that could have been talking about the weather. "And see that you keep her that way. At least until we get her to the warehouse and set everything up."

"What about the street cameras?" asked the second man.

"Taken care of," came the distant voice, "but only for five minutes. That's how long it takes to reset three times. I'll have to end the block then. Any more and a repair alert will be recorded on the Teev database."

"Grab her," said the man with the guttural voice.

Reese peered between her shuttered lids and saw two sets of arms reaching for her. The bare, hairy ones came from the direction of the thug with the guttural voice. He was a strong man with a full beard—one that wasn't CORE approved because of identification issues. The second man's arms were thin but clad in a black jacket, his curved fingers looking like wicked hooks angling her way. His entire frame had the gaunt, hungry look that reminded her of the inmates of Colony 6. His eyes were small and mean.

The hands touched her.

She rolled, kicked out, and found solid flesh. The hairy man grunted in pain. She tried to bounce to her feet, but her wounded shoulder hit the stair behind her. A new wave of agony spread through her body. She clamped her teeth over the moan that threatened to escape. Gathering her strength, she forced herself to roll again.

She caught the briefest glimpse of the third man still down on the sidewalk, watching them with a dispassionate expression. Her glimpse of the man was interrupted as a fist met her face, though from which of her attackers, she didn't know. More kicks rained down on her legs and stomach. She managed to reach her stunner, and fired, but the dart missed. The man with the hairy arms leapt on top of her, his considerable weight smashing her stomach as he calmly punched her face. Blood spurted out her nose. The next punch was to her left eye. The other man continued to kick her side again and again as she was pinned to the steps. She felt the bones in her left hand splinter.

Someone laughed as she moaned. Hairy-arms punched her again in the face. More crunching sounds. Sketches came to her from one of the men, rapid flashes of two other attacks: a helpless woman in a red skirt and a blue-suited man with his mouth open in a scream. Bile rose in her throat.

Then, as if at some unseen signal, the beating stopped. Rough hands pulled her to her feet. Or tried to. Her feet and legs wouldn't carry her, so the men dragged her down the stairs, not seeming to care what their treatment did to her ankles.

Her left eye was swelling shut, but she could see a black

shuttle waiting at the curb behind her scrambler. The third man stood near the shuttle, watching them approach, his shoulder-length hair appearing black under the dim light of the street lamp. He wore a gray outfit and a long black coat open to reveal an under-the-shoulder holster.

She needed to get to her weapons—and fast. If she wanted to survive. Her feet finally righted under her, the adrenaline of the thought giving her legs energy. She ignored the pain as the impact of stepping on the sidewalk reverberated throughout her entire body.

Hands as hard as iron patted down her left side, finding her stunner. It would be of no use to him with the fingerprint release, but without it, her chances of escape were that much lower. Not that her broken fingers on her left hand could have pulled any trigger. She fought the urge to curl into a miserable ball and die.

She fought because that was what they wanted—for her to give up.

She had no doubt they had been sent by Grogovit and the KC. Or maybe his advocate. It didn't matter which. Obviously, someone didn't want her to testify in the morning. And it was also obvious that they planned to kill her. The damage they'd already done was more than a simple scare. They might want her alive for the moment, but not for long. And she was pretty sure that meant her limbs and other parts of her were optional.

More hands patted her right side, finding the nine mil. She grabbed a digit with her right hand, twisting and snapping it. A high, nasal scream met her effort. "My thumb!" the second thug screamed, "The pus bag whore broke my thumb!"

At least she'd done that much.

Still holding her arm in a blood-blocking grip, the hairy man drew back his bulky arm, his face twisting with rage on behalf of his companion. The blow landed on the side of her head, sending her crumpling to the sidewalk. Blood spattered over the ground. Hairy-arms jumped on top of her, pulling back his fist again. If his meaty fist hit her with all that fury behind the blow and with the sidewalk under her head, his boss's command to keep her alive would have no meaning. Maybe it already didn't. Reese jerked her head to the side, and his fist hit the cement. He howled with anger.

She had to survive. At least five minutes. At least until the warning about the non-working street camera was recorded in the Teev feed. Whatever condition she was in, she had to survive that long.

The fingers of her right hand touched the tip of her hidden knife. For long seconds, she fumbled on the hilt. Hairy-arms landed another hit, this time glancing off the side of her head. She lost her grip on the knife. Black edged her vision.

"Enough!" the third man growled. "Get her to the shuttle. Now!"

Where was the knife?

Then her fingers had it. The familiar hilt was in her hands, and instinct took over. Instinct born and bred in Colony 6 and honed as an enforcer. Only her knife was far better than the stolen metal fork she'd used as a child.

She plunged it upward and sideways at Hairy-arms. The knife entered the side of his neck with a wet, satisfying pop. Hairy's face froze, and his hands, reaching for her, fell to his side. He toppled over her, his chest landing on her face.

Reese heaved him off, even as the other two men lunged in her direction. She was free! In horrible, wrenching pain, but free.

In three steps, she was at her scrambler, the controls leaping to life under her handprint. The engine roared and she was off. Bullets pinged off the scrambler, and pain bit into the back of her uniformed left leg as one hit her there.

She wavered a bit as the vision in her remaining functional eye blurred. She blinked furiously. Behind her, the roar of an engine followed. She glanced down at the display that showed the road behind her and saw that the black shuttle was following. Even as she stared, a gun emerged from a window. Shots whizzed past her. The display on her scrambler shattered and went dead. But the scrambler, on manual override, didn't falter.

She pressed the scrambler further, the engine whining with effort. She should be able to lose the shuttle, but somehow it kept up. *Not regulation issue,* she guessed. For a time, she sped nearly blind through the streets before she realized where she was heading. To her partner. To Bay. He was closer than division.

She gasped as a bullet slammed into her back. She fell forward on the scrambler, trying to find breath, trying to stay balanced. Surely some of the passing cameras would catch the shooting. Why wasn't she hearing sirens of rescue?

Unless the third man was interrupting cameras as they went. The power behind that kind of technology made a sob rise in her throat. She had to get to Bay!

Spying a park, she angled her scrambler up on the sidewalk and over the pathways through the lush garden. A stairway of marble steps beckoned her ahead. She gunned the scrambler, nearly losing her seat as it angled up the stairs. There, she'd lost them for now.

"Call Bay," she said to the iTeev on her sleeve. No response. The thugs must have smashed it.

The pain in her torso had dulled slightly, but her responses were slow, her left hand nearly useless, and as she came to a stop outside Bay's apartment building, the scrambler tilted sideways and fell on her wounded left leg. She gritted her teeth against the pain and dragged her leg out, feeling the warmth of blood gushing under her uniform. At least the snug material would help hold in the flow for now. The leg wouldn't hold her weight, though, so she half hopped, half dragged herself up the stairs to Bay's building. A thin light inside the lobby beckoned her. Somehow, she brought herself upright near the glass door. Her right handprint lit up the panel.

"Bay Danvers," she said. "It's Reese. Open up. I'm hurt."

The Teev would alert Bay of her arrival, and he'd signal the door to open for her. Seconds ticked by. "Hurry," she muttered. The door wavered in front of her, and she didn't know how long she could stay conscious. She needed her partner.

There was no response. Where was Bay?

The roar of an engine made her glance over her shoulder at the street. The black shuttle hurtled in her direction.

How did they know where she'd gone?

Still no answer at the door. Why wasn't Bay responding?

Thoughts filtered through her head with blinding quickness. Bay hadn't helped her at the drug bust; he'd only detained nine employees, all of which came down sick. He hadn't wanted to go out on their usual rounds or for their Friday night dinner.

Her stomach seemed to drop from her body. Drop and drop and drop and never end. Was Bay a part of the KC conspiracy?

The black shuttle screeched to a stop. This was it. Reese couldn't fight anymore. She could barely breathe.

Without warning, the door in front of her gave way and she was falling inside. Arms reached out to catch her. She heard a spray of bullets.

Then everything went dark.

CHAPTER 8

The first thing Reese became aware of was the urge to sketch. Images pressed in on her until they filled her entire brain with need. She tried looking around her, to see where she was and if her drawing pad was near, but the room around her was dark. Her limbs refused to move.

The vague thought that she might be dead filtered through her mind, but her next sensation was pain—and lots of it. Her head, her face, her chest, her back, and her legs. Everything hurt. So, not death. At least not yet. Had the KC captured her?

"She might be coming to," came a woman's soft, comforting voice. Reese clung to the sound and tried to follow it back to consciousness.

That was when Reese realized her eyes were closed. With effort, she pulled them open. Or at least one of them; the other eyelid would only lift partway. Light poured in from at least one window, making her blink until her eyes adjusted. The blurry world around her slowly came into partial focus.

"Hey sleepyhead."

The familiar teasing voice came from an indistinct figure to her left. Bay. She squinted and finally recognized the face of her partner. What was he doing here? Had he helped capture her? Somewhere in the room, a monitor began a furious beeping.

"Easy now," came the woman's voice again. A gentle hand touched her right arm. "You're safe, Detective Parker. Your partner got you to us in time. You've undergone a couple surgeries, and we were worried there for a while, but you're going to be all right. You're safe."

Safe. Reese let out a breath she hadn't realized she was holding. The monitor stopped its squealing. She blinked more until the room came into better focus. Unable to move her neck, she rotated her eyes in the direction of the female voice, seeing a woman dressed in a white uniform, her dark hair pulled severely back into a twist. A nurse then.

"That's better," the nurse said. "Now I'll leave you two alone, but only for five minutes. I'm going to get the doctor. He'll want to see how you're doing." To Bay, she added. "Try not to upset her."

Reese waited until the nurse left the room before meeting Bay's gaze. "How long?" Her whisper was hoarse.

"You've been here three weeks." As usual, Bay's big face was flushed, but today his brown eyes glistened with uncharacteristic moisture. "We were beginning to worry that you wouldn't wake up at all. You don't know how glad I am to see you with your eyes open."

"What happened?"

A line appeared between his brow. "You showed up on my doorstep, more dead than not. My stupid door release wasn't working—you know how these pre-Breakdown things always go on the blink—so I went down to let you in and barely opened the door as some guys were getting out of a black shuttle. They had guns. I got you inside, and they took off. We think it was the KC, but we have no proof."

"Had to be them."

"I agree. They obviously didn't want you testifying." Bay reached up and fingered something out of his eye. "I'm really sorry, Reese. I was worried, but not enough, at least not about you. I was thinking of Letisha and the baby. I wanted to stay out of it."

His confession explained his strange behavior that last day. "And Grogovit?" she rasped.

Bay's mouth twisted. "Still in custody. But his case is on hold. I'm sure now that you're awake, they'll pick up proceedings again." He paused before rushing on. "There's more. During the time when we weren't sure you'd make it, information about a drug warehouse was sent anonymously to division. It claimed you were responsible for the drugs, and that you'd framed Grogovit. They had some of your personal belongings and messages that apparently came from you."

"But I—" Reese began.

"I know. It's planted data. They were trying to make it look like you were guilty before killing you. Probably in a fire. You ended all that when you managed to escape." Here he allowed himself a tiny smile. "You're a star, Reese. I mean that in a big way. They're waiting to question you to put it all to rest, of course, but there's nothing to worry about because Captain Homer and I have plenty of solid evidence to support your testimony. And I've made multiple copies of everything proving your innocence. No way is it going to be corrupted this time."

Emotion rushed through Reese, but a flash of a sketch from Bay squashed it as she very clearly saw an image of her own bleeding body in the lobby of his apartment building. The urge to sketch went from a pressing need to a desperate one.

"I need paper," Reese told Bay. "I saw them."

Bay glanced over at her left hand. "They broke your hand in five places, as well as about ten other bones in your body. They've used nanobots to repair a lot of it, but you know how rare those are. Even so, you're still a mess. You need to rest."

He didn't understand that she wouldn't be able to rest until she put the sketches on paper. That was the way her gift—or her curse—worked.

"I'll use my other hand. Then you can find them."

"Look, I'm not kidding. That can wait." He turned and fumbled around on the counter behind him and came up with a mirror, shoving it in front of her.

Reese blinked at the unrecognizable face in the mirror. Her entire head was swathed with bandages and her neck was in some kind of brace. Her skin was more green and black than flesh-colored. At least seven nasty cuts marred her face.

"Luckily with pre-Breakdown tech, you shouldn't have much scarring," he said.

She looked away from the mirror. "I don't care about that. I want to get these guys down on paper while I still remember them. Please."

Bay sighed and put away the mirror, a rueful grin coming to his lips. "Okay. I'll be right back. The little pad you carry in your suit was ruined, so I'll have to pick one up at division. And don't worry while I'm gone. There are always two guards posted outside the door."

Reese hadn't even considered that she'd still be in danger. "I also want you to send a message to the Magistrate Assistant. Tell her I want to testify."

"What?" Bay approached the bed, acting as if he was going to reach out to her but stopping before touching her. Which was a good thing because he was sending her more mental sketches, this time of Grogovit's sick employees. She hadn't known he'd gone to see them in the hospital.

"As soon as I testify, they won't need to hurt me," she insisted.

"Unless they're big on revenge."

That was true, but she hadn't survived for nothing.

"Do it or I will," she said, though there was no way she'd be getting up from that bed anytime soon.

If the Magistrate was still willing to hear her testimony, they might have to wheel her to the administration building to testify. What if the KC was lying in wait?

She pushed the thoughts away. She couldn't think about that now.

As promised, Bay was back in short order with a stack of drawing pads from her office. Reese immediately directed him to put a pencil in her right hand, and she quickly sketched out the images of the men who had attacked her. Only the third man wasn't distinct, as though her memories of him weren't clear. That was often the difference between drawing an actual memory and a sketch. Sketches didn't fade until she'd put them on paper. Her memories did, especially if she hadn't been able to get a decent look at the guy in the first place.

When she was finished, Bay began running the images through the database using his iTeev. He got a hit on the first two men, but not the third. "They've probably gone under-ground, but we'll put a couple teams on it. We'll get them soon enough."

Reese would have to be satisfied with that, but she knew the third man was the dangerous one, and until she found him, she'd always be looking over her shoulder.

"What about my message to the Director's office?" she asked.

Bay heaved a sigh. "I told the captain, and he sent in your message. I'm guessing you'll hear from them sooner rather than later. Grogovit's partners at Kordell Corp have been making a huge stink about us holding him. But so far Captain Homer and I are the only ones besides the nurse and your doctor who know you're awake. We're keeping that under wraps. Hopefully, the KC won't hear about your recovery until it's too late."

"Thanks." Reese nodded, somehow managing to keep the tears from her eyes until her partner left the room.

With the silence pushing down on her, she thought fleetingly of calling her great-aunt, Theena Parker, who had given her a home after leaving the colony. Reese had left instructions in her division file forbidding them to contact Theena unless she was dead, mostly because Reese hadn't wanted to worry her. She certainly didn't want to give the old lady a fright now. No, she'd wait a few weeks until she could move around better and when more of the visible injuries had faded.

With a resigned sigh and a great deal of effort, Reese pulled her personal notepad out of the stack Bay had set next to her right leg and recorded the two sketches she'd caught from her coworkers before leaving work that fateful Friday, the woman in the red skirt and the blue-suited man that she'd glimpsed from her attackers, Bay's sketches of Grogovit's sick employees, and then finally his image of herself lying on the floor in his lobby.

At last her hand was still and she could rest. The doctor had given her a pain pump, but she hadn't dared use it until she got out the sketches. Now she pressed the button and closed her eyes. After a while, the pain faded. She drifted.

Only moments seemed to have passed when a commotion at the door made her jerk awake. But no, she'd slept for hours, if she could judge by the angle of light streaming through the window. It was near dinnertime maybe. Maybe even dinner-time the next day.

The nurse from before stood in the doorway, two red dots on her cheeks. She looked panicked. Two men in gray suits followed her into the room, each carrying an automatic assault rifle.

Had the KC broken past her guards? Reese looked around for a weapon, but all she had was her pencil. Her monitor began beeping angrily.

"I'm sorry," the nurse said, her voice quick and breathy, "but you have a Visitor." The way she said visitor capitalized the word with great importance. She put out a hand to silence the alarm.

Still clutching her pencil, Reese's eyes fixed on the doorway as a black-robed figure stepped through. There was no mistaking that black mask. "Magistrate," Reese choked out. Her jaw would have gaped open in shock if the bandages around her head would have let it. She was glad she was in bed, or she might have collapsed in disbelief.

Two more gray-suited, armed men behind the Magistrate took up position at the door. "I'm happy you have regained consciousness," the Magistrate said without preamble. She paused, as if waiting for Reese to respond.

"Thank you," Reese choked out.

The Magistrate inclined her head. It was impossible to tell her exact size under the voluminous robes, but she appeared shorter and her shoulders more narrow than they had been on the dais at the administration building.

"I hear you are ready to proceed with your testimony," the Magistrate continued.

"I am, but I didn't think—"

"Given your experience the last time you were scheduled to testify," the Magistrate said, "I thought it best to do this immediately." She waved a hand and the wall next to Reese shimmered to life with a holo display of the chambers at the administration building. Grogovit and his advocate were in attendance, as was the green-robed doctor and two sets of enforcers. The latter were heavily armed, despite the normal no-weapons rule for the judgment chambers.

"Detective Parker, can you please relate the events leading up to discovering the factory, and what happened once you arrived?" the Magistrate asked.

"Yes." Taking a deep breath, Reese began with the first sketch she had made at division while interviewing Cruz, explaining how it had led them to Grogovit's office building, the discussion with the janitor, and finding the factory.

"And how did you happen to have the drawing of the building that was behind the factory?"

"It was a drawing I'd made from an informant earlier," Reese said, which was true, even if Cruz didn't know he'd informed on his boss. "I showed it to him on a whim."

That seemed to satisfy the Magistrate. "Go on."

Reese continued, telling about going into the building and the conversation she'd overheard Grogovit having with his manager. The now-conveniently-dead manager. Reese tried to include details, like the peanut smell and the expressions on the men's faces. Every detail, except for the sketches she saw from other people's minds. She glanced at Grogovit in the holoscreen only a time or two as she spoke. He sat with his arms folded and a confident smile on his puffy lips.

"Grogovit said he was late because he had been planting evidence to incriminate only Cruz," Reese said at the very end of her recitation, "and that as long as everyone at the factory kept their mouths shut, their drug operation would continue."

"Are you absolutely positive that is what he said?" asked the Magistrate.

Reese tried to nod but the bandages wouldn't let her. "Absolutely."

Grogovit's advocate stood, but the Magistrate waved him to silence before he could speak. Silence filled the room.

Had Reese's testimony been enough? Did the Magistrate believe her, or would she sense that she was holding something back?

"Since we last spoke," the Magistrate said, "did you know that Tadum Grogovit's advocate has brought to my attention evidence that implicates you in the manufacture and distribution of juke?"

Reese saw Grogovit exchange a gloating look with his advocate, who had retaken his seat. She opened her mouth to speak, but the Magistrate beat her to it. "Fortunately, your captain has presented more than enough solid evidence to exonerate you. This is not the first time Kordell Corp has been under suspicion, nor the first time they have tried disgraceful tactics to absolve themselves of guilt."

"Magistrate, I must object," protested Grogovit's advocate, once again springing to his feet.

"Enough!" The Magistrate's voice boomed through the room with more power than Reese had ever heard from a person of her stature. "You've had weeks to present evidence, and I've had weeks to think about the case. I am prepared to pass sentence." She paused momentarily before continuing, as if waiting to make sure everyone was listening. "Tadum Grogovit, please rise."

Grogovit's smile was gone now, but he still didn't look afraid. He rose fluidly, as if sure he'd already won. And maybe he had. It was his word against hers. Well, besides the disappearing evidence and people dropping dead like it was Breakdown all over again.

"In light of the very convincing testimony of Enforcer

Parker, and your presence at the factory," the Magistrate intoned without inflection, "I find you guilty of the manufacture and distribution of juke."

Grogovit stared at her, as if unable to believe what he was hearing. He glanced at his advocate, who studiously avoided his gaze.

"Fortunately," the Magistrate continued, her voice softening, "you live in a society that helps those who break the law instead of executing or imprisoning them. We'll get you the help you need, Mr. Grogovit. To that end, I hereby sentence you to medical enhancement. The procedure will take place immediately. Enforcers, please escort your prisoner to the enhancement center."

A gasp escaped Grogovit's lips. Two of the enforcers leapt toward Grogovit, taking both his arms. Grogovit struggled, flailing out at his advocate, as if trying to hit him, but the enforcers pulled him back. The doctor withdrew a hypo from a hidden pocket of his green robe and pushed it against Grogovit's skin, depressing the tip.

Grogovit's head swung toward the doctor. "Why you—" Whatever else he had been going to say was lost as he collapsed, saved from crashing to the floor only by the support of the enforcers.

"I'll have someone with a wheelchair meet you in the hallway," the doctor said.

The two enforcers grunted in response and began dragging Grogovit across the glossy floor to the exit. The other enforcers followed them.

To the advocate, the doctor added, "Please let his family know that they'll be able to see him tomorrow. By then he'll be recovered enough from the operation. They can expect a kinder, more loving version of his former self. Good day." With a nod in the Magistrate's direction, he also took his leave. Only Grogovit's advocate was left, staring sightlessly back at them.

The Magistrate gave a downward wave of her hand and the scene on the wall vanished. "The Director will make the announcement about the sentencing later this afternoon when the enhancement procedure is complete," she said. "Thanks to your survival, Detective Parker, the CORE is now a safer place, and people will think twice about breaking our laws. You are a hero."

Reese felt suddenly weak. It was over. Finally. "Thank you. But if it's okay, I'd rather my name be kept off the Teev. I've had enough excitement."

To her surprise, the Magistrate laughed. "I think that can be arranged. We will also expunge the public record to omit your involvement. That may help keep you safe."

Which meant she wasn't sure Reese wouldn't still be a target, but with Grogovit heading to surgery, the KC would at least have no immediate reason to kill her.

The Magistrate inclined her head and left the room without another word.

With a sigh of relief, Reese closed her eyes and slept.

When she awoke again the next day, Bay was there to let her know that using the identifications made by her drawings, he had found and picked up one of the two men who had attacked her. The hairy man had been found dead in the river. The survivor hadn't implicated the KC in the attack but claimed he and his partner had been after Reese's weapons to sell on the black market.

"They'll be sent to medical enhancement," Bay said. "No doubt. And they don't have money or family, so it's likely they'll live out the rest of their lives working in a colony factory."

"What about the third guy?" Reese asked. "He was the one calling the shots."

Bay shook his head. "We didn't find an ID on him. Yet."

Reese doubted they ever would. She's seen the length to which Kordell Corp had gone to protect their partner, and she suspected that the third man was someone important in the organization.

Not finding him bothered Reese a lot, but there was nothing she could do about it. At least not yet. Nothing but get better—and as fast as she could.

CHAPTER 9

F ive months after the attack, and with more than a dozen
surgeries to her name, Reese was anxious to leave the
hospital and get back to work. She'd been trying to tell Captain
Homer that she was fine for the past month, but he'd kept her
on the rehabilitation floor until she could completely pass her
enforcer medical, which included hand-to-hand combat. There
had been no sign of retribution from the KC, and her security
had lessened to one enforcer. Thanks to Bay, she had a new
Enforce nine mil, as well as a replacement knife.

The public retirement of Kordell Corp executive Tadum
Grogovit had been top news for weeks, but people had eventually moved on. Three months ago, Grogovit had arisen again
briefly in the news when his second child was born, and during
his interview, he looked affable and happy. If his speech was a
little distracted and vague, no one commented on it. Maybe he
couldn't work or make more money, but then he didn't need to.
He wouldn't be making drugs either—that was the important

thing—and he'd be spending a lot more time with his family. Reese tried to put him from her mind.

She still had dreams. Dreams of the attack. Dreams of being enhanced. Dreams of the janitor walking with a cleaner while his mind screamed for release.

Worse, she was beginning to have doubts about the CORE. About their methods of punishment, their tight control, the luxury of the Elite while children fought for their lives in the colonies. But she didn't tell anyone that, of course.

At last, on a Wednesday afternoon, Captain Homer appeared in her room at the hospital to sign her release papers. Bay was with him.

"I was beginning to think you were going to keep me in here forever," she said to the captain. She began folding the clothes Bay had brought for her from her apartment, stuffing them into a bag he'd also retrieved. Getting home would be nice. She was already envisioning being there, especially on the balcony where tonight she'd sit and watch the sunset.

Homer laughed a bit too loudly for the short, rounded man he was. "Of course not. We just want to make sure you'll be good and ready for your next assignment."

Reese's hands stilled. "What do you mean?"

The captain faced her, meeting her gaze. "You're being transferred."

"What. Why?" Reese glanced at Bay, who was staring at his feet.

Captain Homer sighed. "Sorry, Reese, it's just the way it's got to be. For now, anyway. The KC is powerful, and the fact is, no one wants to risk being your partner. You need to transfer far away where others won't be killed when the KC tries to get to you."

"When the KC . . . But they haven't tried anything."

"That's because you've been in here. Under protection.

Unfortunately, that ends today, and there's too many people around here to let you remain a target. It's for your own good."

Reese ignored the captain's words and stared at her partner. "Bay, is this true? You don't want to be my partner?"

Bay sheepishly met her gaze. "I'm going to be a dad. I have to think of the baby."

"And everyone else at division feels the same way?"

He nodded, his eyes once again finding something of interest on the floor.

Anger and disappointment flooded Reese. There was no choice then, not really. She took a deep breath and sat on the bed, staring at her hands. She felt as if someone had shot her in the back. And she knew exactly what that felt like. "Where?" she asked.

"That's the attitude." Homer slapped her on the back. "I knew you'd see reason."

"Where?" she repeated.

"Dallastar Territory. Amarillo City, to be exact. You'll like it there. Stay a couple of years, beat back a few of those radiation-crazed fringers they're always having trouble with, and then if you want, we'll see about bringing you back. The captain there, name of Brogan, is looking forward to talking with you. He'll tell you when to be there. If I were you, though, I might take a bit of a circuitous route on your way there. Just in case. We won't tell anyone where you've gone, of course."

Reese barely heard him. Dallastar. Colony 6 was in Dallastar, and she'd planned never to go back. Every part of her wanted to throw the offer into her captain's face, even if it meant stepping down. Or going to work for the Central Identification Unit. But she couldn't do that. She'd worked too hard to make detective, and this was the only career she knew of that would allow her to make use of the sketches. Besides, the artists at the

CIU were likely just as afraid of retribution from the KC as the enforcers at division.

The one silver lining was that her great-aunt lived only a short sky train ride from Amarillo City. She'd be deliriously happy to see more of Reese, and if Reese were honest, she missed the old woman, her only living relative.

Reese took a deep breath and resumed her packing, ignoring the men who stood awkwardly watching her. She was going back to Dallastar. To the memories. To the guilt. To wondering what happened to her Colony 6 crew.

Maybe it was time to find out.

Teyla Branton grew up avidly reading science fiction and fantasy and watching Star Trek reruns with her large family. They lived on a little farm where she loved to visit the solitary cow and collect (and juggle) the eggs, usually making it back to the house with most of them intact. On that same farm she once owned thirty-three gerbils and eighteen cats, not a good mix, as it turns out. Teyla always had her nose in a book and daydreamed about someday creating her own worlds.

Teyla is now married, mostly grown up, and has seven kids, so life at her house can be very interesting (and loud), but writing keeps her sane. She thrives on the energy and daily amusement offered by her children, the semi-ordered chaos giving her a constant source of writing material. Teyla grabs any bit of free time from her hectic life to write. She's been known to wear pajamas all day when working on a deadline, and is often distracted enough to burn dinner. (Okay, pretty much 90% of the time.)

She loves writing fiction and traveling, and she hopes to write and travel a lot more. She also loves shooting guns, martial arts, and belly dancing. She has worked in the publishing business for over twenty years. Teyla also writes romance and suspense under the name Rachel Branton. For more information or to join her mailing list and get a free ebook, please visit http://www.TeylaBranton.com.

www.ingramcontent.com/pod-product-compliance
Lightning Source LLC
Chambersburg PA
CBHW070638130626
46555CB00006B/2599